There were several computers set up on the second floor

The stations were all empty, and Audrey sat down in front of one, thankful that no one was here today.

She put one hand on the keyboard, anxiety making her nearly light-headed. She blinked it away, logged on to the account she had set up under a fake name, clicked on Write Mail and typed in the address she had memorized. Several minutes passed before she could bring herself to type the words. Doing so felt like jumping off a cliff, with no guarantee of ever hitting bottom.

Hello. I am told you might be able to help me.

Dear Reader,

Audrey Colby is a woman who took a wrong turn early in her life. Ignored that little voice of doubt that bid her to take a second look. We've all done it. It's just that some bad decisions put us in worse places than others.

Like most of the choices we make, the picture isn't black and white. Audrey has a son whom she loves heart and soul. And she's determined to give him the life he deserves, a life free of the awful things he's seen from his father.

I once heard someone living in a difficult situation asked why she stayed, why she didn't leave. Her answer? "At least this devil I know."

That's the tough part. Prying ourselves out of the familiar, even when it's bad, and flinging ourselves into the unknown.

I think of my own life as a tapestry, countless threads of good and bad woven together. It would be impossible to pull one thread without changing the landscape of the entire thing, making it something other than what it is. Maybe the challenge then is to find peace with the choices we've made, and go forward with experience as a beacon to light our path.

I love to hear from readers. Please visit my Web site at www.inglathcooper.com. Or write to me at P.O. Box 973, Rocky Mount, VA 24151.

All best,

Inglath Cooper

A Year and a Day
Inglath Cooper

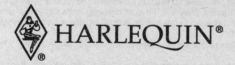

TORONTO • NEW YORK • LONDON
AMSTERDAM • PARIS • SYDNEY • HAMBURG
STOCKHOLM • ATHENS • TOKYO • MILAN • MADRID
PRAGUE • WARSAW • BUDAPEST • AUCKLAND

ISBN 0-373-71310-X

A YEAR AND A DAY

Copyright © 2005 by Inglath Cooper.

Printed in U.S.A.

Books by Inglath Cooper

HARLEQUIN SUPERROMANCE

Don't miss any of our special offers. Write to us at the following address for information on our newest releases.

Harlequin Reader Service
U.S.: 3010 Walden Ave., P.O. Box 1325, Buffalo, NY 14269
Canadian: P.O. Box 609, Fort Erie, Ont. L2A 5X3

For my husband, Mac, and my daughters, Kavvi, Tatti and Nadia. You make my life complete.

CHAPTER ONE

AUDREY COLBY HATED New Year's Eve.

It was the one day of the year when people celebrated the old and ushered in the new, the turning of the calendar an impossible-to-deny reminder of another twelve months slipping by. One more year, and nothing had changed. Or rather, she had changed nothing.

She sat in front of the walnut vanity, the reflection in the heavy Venetian mirror barely recognizable. With one finger, she traced the now faded bruise just beneath her jaw. She opened a drawer and pulled out a tube of concealer, dotted some on and smoothed it in. The yellow-green shadow surrendered temporarily, nearly invisible.

"Audrey, are you ready?" Her husband's voice echoed up from downstairs. Smooth. Cultured. Tainted by a hint of irritation.

The muscles in her stomach tightened. But outwardly she showed no emotion. She'd grown used to the bland stranger in the mirror. The woman who never smiled, whose eyes were flat and life-less. She considered not finishing her makeup. Did it really matter how much she put on, any-way? She'd still hate the way she looked. She could see past the mask, after all. Even if the rest of the world couldn't.

Footsteps sounded on the stairs. Jonathan ap-peared in the doorway, one shoulder propped against the frame. He wore a black tuxedo, his face tan against a starched white shirt, his expres-sion placid. "What's taking so long?" he asked. "We're late."

Audrey forced herself to meet her husband's gaze, strove for a note of reason in her voice. "Why don't you go without me tonight? I'm not feeling well."

He crossed the room, lifted a strand of her hair and wrapped it around his finger. Something flick-ered in his brown eyes. "I can't do that," he said. "What would people think?"

"What does it matter what people think?"

"Ross and Sylvia are expecting us," he said, his tone matter-of-fact.

A sudden furnace of anger ignited inside her. "And Laura?" Amazingly enough, her voice re-mained even.

He went still, raised an eyebrow, a half smile touching his mouth. "I believe Ross said she's still in from school. Since when are you so interested in seeing Laura?"

Audrey's fury collapsed as quickly as it had erupted. "I'm not," she said, her voice neutral. Sammy was in his room, watching a DVD. She didn't want him to hear their raised voices.

She rose from the stool and walked to her closet, a small room in itself, the light snapping on automatically when she opened the door. She closed her eyes and fought back the hopelessness pressing down on her. Again and again, they danced the same dance, their lives stuck on this one loop. Go along to get along.

But she had a plan. A way out. And for now, that was all that mattered. A plan. It would get her through. She clung to the thought of it like a drowning woman to a single buoy.

"Audrey?" Jonathan stood at the closet entrance, an edge to his voice now.

"I should finish getting ready," she said, flipping through the dresses, taking one from the rack without looking at it.

Jonathan yanked it from her hand, tossed it on the floor like it was garbage, then pulled her to him. He lowered his head, kissing the side of her jaw where the bruise was now disguised, then the tip of her chin, and finally, her mouth. "So beautiful," he said, drawing back to look at her. "I keep thinking that one day, I'll look at you and see you in a different light. So far, no."

Bird in a cage, she thought. What pretty feathers. A snap of the fingers, and the bird sings.

"By the way," he said, close to her ear, "I thought you'd like to know I've made arrangements for Samuel to begin at the Cade Country School."

The words hit her like a brick to the chest. For a moment, she felt as if all the air in her lungs had been forced out. She couldn't breathe. A hand to her throat, she said, "What do you mean you've made arrangements?"

"A boarding school in Connecticut," he explained rationally, as if there were anything even remotely rational in what he was saying. "They'll have a room available for him mid-February. The school is completing new housing, and they're willing to take him in to the semester. We'll plan to fly him up after my trip to the Dominican Republic."

Audrey stared at him, too stunned to respond. When she finally found her voice, it didn't sound like her own. "Sammy isn't going anywhere. He can't. He's too young—"

"He's nine years old," Jonathan said abruptly. "Cade starts with fourth graders. I think it would do him good to have some time away from you.

You've made him far too clingy. It's time he stopped being such a mama's boy."

She wrapped her arms around her waist, as if she could somehow hold back the sudden avalanche of pain tumbling through her. She had long ago learned that arguing with Jonathan was an exercise in futility. She bit her lip now to keep from screaming at him.

He stepped forward, pushing her aside. She stumbled, righted herself with a hand on the wall. He rummaged through the clothes, impatient, pulling a black dress from a hanger and throwing it at her. "Wear this," he said. "The other one looks cheap."

She took the dress into the bathroom, a too-familiar and equally impotent anger rising like bile in her throat. She forced it back, refusing to waste the energy. Instead, she would focus on the immediate future, on how to make her plan happen sooner, her mind suddenly buzzing with the steps that would need to be completed.

She had the e-mail address. All she had to do was use it.

Tomorrow. She would start tomorrow. This time, it would happen. This time, there was no other choice.

THE SURPRISE PARTY wasn't much of a surprise.

Nicholas Wakefield supposed he should be

grateful his colleagues in the Atlanta District Attorney's office had chosen to send him off with good wishes instead of rotten apples.

The apples would have been more appropriate, considering how difficult he'd been to live with the past couple of months.

All the same, he wished they had skipped the party. Leaving this place was going to be hard enough without having to put a happy face on it.

From the hall just outside his office came muffled whispers mingled with laughter. The sooner he went in, the sooner it would be over. He sighed and forced his feet to move.

"Surprise!"

The greeting exploded in front of him, followed by a few grumbles about how long it had taken him to get back from the file room.

"A man could get arthritis stooped over for that long," Kyle Travers said, shaking his head. Kyle had a barrel-size chest and a voice to match. As district attorney, he used it whenever he needed to play the intimidation card. "Get in here, Nicholas, and cut this cake," he boomed.

Nicholas walked over to the table and picked up the knife. "You bake this yourself?"

"From scratch." Kyle smiled, slapping him on the back. "Amy did. And she said to make sure you actually eat some of it."

"You're married to one of Atlanta's best cooks. Anything she fixes, I'll eat." Nicholas looked around the room at the faces he'd grown to know so well over the past nine years. For the most part, they were a good bunch. Some, he'd actually miss working with. Kyle, most of all. The two of them shared a common philosophy on how the system should work, and a mutual disgust for the fact that more often than not, it didn't.

"You shouldn't have done this," Nicholas said to the smiling group.

"So change your mind about leaving, and we'll take down all the balloons, eat the cake and pretend this little surprise party never happened." This from Eleana Elliott, Kyle's secretary. She leaned against a file cabinet in the far corner of the office, looking out at him over a pair of the kind of sturdy black-framed glasses that made smart people look smarter.

Murmurs of agreement rippled through the room.

Kyle held up a hand. "Let's not start that again," he said. "Nicholas is going civilian. Quit giving him a hard time about it. This is supposed to be a party. So cut the cake, Wakefield."

Someone cranked the volume on a boom box, Outkast rattling the ceiling tiles, the mood of the party instantly lifting. A few people started dancing.

Nicholas made his way through the crowd,

thanking everyone for their congratulations on his new job, reluctant though some of them were to see him leave. Part of him appreciated that most of the people here didn't want to see him go. Another part of him knew he had to. For his own sanity, he couldn't stay.

An hour later, someone blared a request for more cups. Nicholas volunteered to get them, glad for the momentary escape. In the hallway, the din of music and voices lowered a decibel or two. He went in the office next door, found the cups behind the desk, then sat in the chair and leaned back, closing his eyes. They wouldn't miss him for a few minutes. In tying up the last loose ends of his responsibilities here, he'd averaged four hours of sleep a night for the past few nights, most of them on the couch in his office. He was bone-tired.

"Hey, you know I don't really want you to go either."

Nicholas looked up. Kyle stood in the doorway, one beefy shoulder against the jamb. "You'll just miss my coffeemaking skills."

Kyle rolled his eyes. "Anybody can do a to-go cup from Starbucks."

"Yeah, but I get it the way you like it."

"True." Kyle came in and sat down in the chair across from the desk, his hands behind his head.

"So what's your plan? Find a good woman? Settle down?"

Nicholas propped one elbow on the side of the chair. "I'm not complaining about the status quo."

"The status quo's fine for a Saturday-night diversion, but that bed's got to get a little chilly the rest of the week."

"Hadn't noticed."

Kyle snorted. "One of these days, you're going to."

"I do better solo. And besides, I don't want to be responsible for anyone except myself."

"Sounds lonely if you ask me."

Nicholas let that one go. He couldn't deny that sometimes, it was.

Kyle was silent for a few moments, and then said, "Maybe it's a good thing you're getting out of this place. Since your first day here, you've taken the weight of every case that comes across your desk as if your own salvation depended on the outcome."

"Maybe it did," Nicholas said softly.

Kyle blew out a sigh, fatigue edging out the previous cheer in his expression. "We did everything we could for that little girl, Nick. You know that."

The words hung between them. Since the verdict, this was the first reference either of them had made to the case. Nicholas sat up in the desk chair. "Yeah. So I keep telling myself."

"We did."

"I got too comfortable," he said, his voice low. "Let myself think we had the case wrapped up tight. And because of it, that crazy bastard got off scot-free."

"The jury didn't buy it, man."

"She was just a kid," Nicholas said, suddenly weary. Fourteen. Even younger than his sister. He broke the thought off there, a batch of bad memories assaulting him.

Kyle sighed, his tone measured when he said, "You think it doesn't kill me to see scum like Dayton slide through the cracks? I do all I can within the realm of the system, and at least that's something."

There it was. The implication that Nicholas was selling out. But then, wasn't that exactly what he was doing?

Nine years ago, he had started out in the prosecutor's office on fire with the need to make a difference. Just over a month ago, he'd finally admitted to himself that when it came right down to it, he hadn't changed anything.

The disappointment of that clung to him, invisible, choking.

With the verdict in the Mary-Ellen Moore case, reality had hit him. He couldn't do the job anymore. A switch inside him had been permanently shut off. He woke up every morning certain that all the old energy, the passion he'd once felt for his work would have returned.

But the more he yearned for that old fire, the more it seemed to evade him.

He couldn't forget the girl's face. The crime-scene photos revealing with sickening accuracy her innocence. Lips parted as if she had been shocked to discover that the world could end up so ugly. Her dress torn. One sandal missing. The last image of his little sister all those years ago flashed through his mind, sending a knife of pain through his gut. He ran a hand over his eyes.

"I promised that family," he said. "I promised them that son of a bitch would pay."

"Nicholas—"

"But that was my mistake, wasn't it? Never make promises you can't keep, right?" He grabbed the cups and stood. "We better get back out there. I've got another party to go to."

"Yeah," Kyle said, slapping his hands on his knees and pushing out of his chair. "Wouldn't want to keep your new employer waiting."

Nicholas attempted a smile. "First impressions and all that."

Kyle squeezed his shoulder once. "Miss us a little, will ya?"

"I don't think I'll have a choice."

AUDREY AND JONATHAN arrived at the Websters'
just after nine o'clock. She could think of nothing
but Jonathan's intention to send Sammy away,
and she wished simply for the evening to be over,
to be alone with her thoughts long enough to reassure herself that her plan would work.

A who's who roster of cars—Bentleys, BMWs,
Ferraris—lined the driveway outside the West
Paces Ferry mansion. Spotlights held the enormous house captive in their glare. Thomas stopped
the car in the circular drive and opened the back
door of the Mercedes limousine. Jonathan slid
out, offering her a hand. She ignored it. His frown
lasted only a millisecond, replaced with a pleasant smile directed at the chauffeur.

"I'll call your cell phone when we're ready to
leave, Thomas," he said.

Thomas nodded. "Yes, sir."

Jonathan put a possessive arm around Audrey's
waist and pulled her close, forcing her to walk
next to him. This was the part he'd perfected. The
Colbys. Happily married couple. Adoring husband. Pampered wife.

Ross and Sylvia Webster stood in the doorway.
A former weight lifter who had let the muscle go
soft, Ross wore suits that were a shade tight, as if
he couldn't quite admit to needing to go up a size.
A couple of inches taller than her husband, Syl-

via was a study in elegance, her dark hair loosely pulled back with a diamond clip, her red silk dress fitted to every aerobicized curve.

One of the premier houses in Atlanta, the Webster home contained an indoor pool, racketball courts and a huge ballroom in which the party took place. Proof that silence was lucrative.

"Hello, Jonathan. Audrey." Ross shook Jonathan's hand, then reached down to brush his lips across Audrey's cheek. His gaze caught hers, but he quickly looked away, avoiding her eyes while Jonathan greeted Sylvia.

Sylvia laughed at something Jonathan had whispered in her ear, then turned to Audrey. "Let's get you something to drink, and I'll tell you all about the fabulous new designer I found. I think his stuff would look great on you."

"I'll watch for you," Jonathan called out, his voice low and even.

Audrey followed the other woman through the foyer. Red poinsettias lined the stairway. Garlands of magnolia leaves hung from the banister, draping the entrance to the ballroom. Bottles of Dom Perignon and crystal glasses caught the light from the chandeliers suspended overhead. A tuxedo-clad singer crooned a Sinatra tune, an orchestra set up behind him.

"Love the coat," Sylvia said, rubbing a hand across the sleeve of Audrey's mink.

"Thanks." Audrey handed it to a hovering butler. She despised it. Despised herself more for wearing it when the thought of killing an animal for its fur had always repulsed her. But she mostly hated the coat because it had been one of Jonathan's extravagant apologies. One of many.

Sylvia passed her a glass of champagne. "Missed you at the League fashion show yesterday. Some of the cruisewear was simply to die for."

Audrey took a sip, not meeting the other woman's eyes. "Really?"

Sylvia made a sound of disapproval. "I wish I could afford to be as unconcerned as you. But then you could put on a sack and look great in it."

Audrey wondered what Sylvia would have said if she told her what she saw when she looked in the mirror. "Did you find anything for your trip to St. Barts?" she asked, forcing herself to make an effort at polite conversation.

Sylvia brightened. "A few things, but I'm really excited about the Martin Hospice show on the second. You're still planning to go, right?"

Actually, she'd forgotten about it. Jonathan had brought home the invitation, suggested she go with Sylvia. It was good to be seen at such events. She would have preferred to make an anonymous donation, but that would have been wasting an opportunity for public credit. "I—yes," she said.

"Of course, it's a charity show, but I understand Neiman's has held back some of their spring items to donate."

"How nice," Audrey said.

Sylvia went on to tell her about the Dolce & Gabbana swimsuit Carol Estings had all but ripped from her hand last week at Saks.

Audrey made the appropriate sounds of interest, all the while wishing she could fast-forward the next few hours. Get past the night's inevitable conclusion. Even if she stood in a corner by herself, there was always a trigger. A passing waiter who smiled her way. A married man asking directions to the bathroom.

It didn't have to make sense. It rarely did. The conclusion was inevitable.

CHAPTER TWO

NICHOLAS STOOD on the fringe of the Websters' party, reminding himself he needed to mingle. As the most recently hired partner at Webster & Associates, working the crowd for future clients was the reason he'd been invited here tonight.

But he was out of his element. And then some.

Surrounding him were the elite of Atlanta society. CEOs lamenting the Dow-Jones. A lawyer bragging about the workhorse of a paralegal he'd just hired. A local actress touting her most recent chemical peel.

He'd left the surprise party at the office and driven home to change. He glanced down at his newly purchased tuxedo, wondered if it looked as wrong on him as it felt. He'd never been a tuxedo kind of guy, but then he'd never imagined himself going to work for one of the biggest corporate law firms in the city either.

Things changed.

People changed.

He let his gaze wander the room, noticing two women who, like him, stood at the edge of the crowd, talking. On the left, Sylvia Webster. They'd met a few days ago in Ross's office. Nice enough, if a little eager to please where her husband was concerned.

The woman beside her looked familiar, but he couldn't place where he'd seen her. Beautiful. But there was something else in her face that made him look closer. The impression that like him, she might be tolerating the party rather than enjoying it.

He glanced at her left hand. A wedding ring gleamed in the light.

"There you are, Nicholas." Ross Webster wound his way around a few people, leaving space for the man who followed closely behind. "I want you to meet one of our most important clients. Jonathan Colby, this is Nicholas Wakefield, our newest partner at W&A."

Colby stuck out his hand, his grip firm, authoritative. An inch or two under six feet, he had the stature of a man clearly used to having other people's attention. He reminded Nicholas of a stallion he'd seen with a group of mares on a trip out west when he was a boy. With a look, that stallion had made his position clear to any would-be encroachers. Dared them to challenge him.

"Good to meet you, Nicholas," he said, his voice smooth and welcoming.

"Pleasure, Mr. Colby. I'm looking forward to working with you."

"Jonathan, please. I would say you're in for a big change from high crimes and misdemeanors."

"I'm counting on it," Nicholas said.

"We'll have plenty to keep you busy." Colby held his gaze for a moment, then smiled and mentioned some of the things they had in the works, a pending lawsuit with a company out of Savannah and a couple other things that sounded tame enough. But then that was exactly what Nicholas had signed on for, wasn't it?

Tame.

AUDREY STOOD at one end of the Websters' massive living room, an upbeat Cole Porter tune plucking at her sensitized nerves.

Sylvia had excused herself to check with the caterer on the champagne levels, and Audrey was glad to escape her questioning eyes.

She glanced around for Jonathan.

A few minutes ago, he'd been standing by the bar talking to Ross and a younger man she did not recognize.

She caught sight of Jonathan at the foot of the

curved marble staircase. He adjusted his bowtie, then took the stairs two at a time.

Her lungs seized with the need for air. She weaved her way to the back of the house and pushed out the French doors into the night.

LAURA WEBSTER STOOD in the middle of her childhood bedroom, halfway through her second glass of wine. Ridiculously enough, the room was still pink and white, her old toys neatly arranged on the shelves next to her bed.

She glanced at her watch. He was late. They'd agreed to meet at ten-thirty. Nearly an hour ago.

Patience had never been one of her strong suits.

Laura hated to be kept waiting. As an only child, her life to date had been one of immediate gratification, and she wasn't very adept at handling anything less. Both her parents generally fell over themselves making sure her every need was met.

And she had a lot of needs. Most recently, a fondness for Prada, which she'd indulged during a weekend trip to Manhattan, maxing out her platinum Visa.

Her dad obviously hadn't gotten the bill yet. All of his blood vessels were still intact.

But then giving her stuff made her parents happy. They were the ones who'd set it up that way. No, Laura, we can't make it to your horse show this weekend, but if you do well, we'll talk about that new pony.

They'd taught her the payoff system early in life. And she had always been a good student.

She moved to the dresser, picked up a sable powder brush and flicked it over nose and chin, studying herself in the mirror, liking what she saw. Small nose, full mouth, chin-length dark hair with subtle highlights courtesy of Madison Avenue's Jean-Paul. When she walked by, men looked. A date tonight would have been a non-issue, and yet here she stood, waiting.

A knock sounded at the door.

Laura picked up her wineglass, and cleared her expression of everything but indifference. "Come in."

The door opened. She hadn't turned on a lamp, and for a moment, Jonathan was illuminated by the light from the hallway. He stepped inside, closed the door behind him. "I'd given up on you."

"Sorry," he said, but didn't look it.

She tamped down her irritation, refusing to let it show. She'd wanted him since she was sixteen years old. Had started flirting with him at her parents' parties, a brush of the arm here, a lingering look there. Teasing him had been like tossing a match at the edge of a streak of gasoline, hoping it would strike and yet clueless as to how to put the fire out if it did.

It had taken six years for her efforts to finally burst into full flame. Sometimes, she wasn't sure if she could handle what she'd gotten herself into. But she did like trying.

She crossed the room, slipped her hand inside his white shirt.

"I don't have long," he said, looking down at her with a flare of heat in his eyes.

Laura liked that.

She slid the strap of her dress off one shoulder, then the other. It fell to the floor. Beneath, she wore nothing.

His mouth found the curve of her throat, teeth nipping just behind her ear.

There were no lights on in the room, but the curtains were open, and noise drifted up from the party. He backed her closer to the window, kissing her so hard that she felt a bruise bloom on her mouth.

Anyone who looked up could have clearly seen them.

Laura liked that, too.

NICHOLAS'S SOCIAL SKILLS could be classified as rusty at best, and, with another half hour to go before midnight, he headed out one of the doors at the back of the house, intent on a few minutes of solitude. A slate terrace took up much of the yard. Round white tables with matching chairs were scattered across the expanse of it, umbrellas planted in the center of each one. A set of wide stone steps led away from the lit-up house.

Three-quarters of the way down, he saw her. Her hair was a pale blond, straight, parted in the middle. It grazed the curve of her shoulder. Diamond earrings matched the one on her left hand in size.

Compared to the plunging necklines most of the women had worn here tonight, her dress rated conservative. Understated though it was, it failed to conceal the curves of her body. She had a quiet elegance that was undeniably appealing.

He recognized her then. Recalled a newspaper photo of her at some fund-raiser.

Colby. Audrey Colby.

He should go back inside.

Nicholas had always trusted his intuition. It was almost never wrong.

But he ignored the voice of reason now. Something stronger pulled him across the terrace, as if he'd been drawn by some magnetic force field.

She looked up and took a step back. "I'm sorry," he said. "I didn't mean to scare you."

"I didn't hear you," she said, one hand at her throat.

He slid one finger around the rim of his shirt

collar. "It was getting a little stuffy in there. The air feels good."

"Yes, it does," she agreed after a few seconds. She watched him for a moment, then said, "Excuse me," before stepping past him toward the steps that led to the house.

Again, that voice. Let her go. "You're Jonathan Colby's wife, aren't you?"

She stopped on the third step, her back to him, pausing before she half turned, silent.

"I'm Nicholas Wakefield," he added. "Ross just hired me. I'll be working with your husband."

She stared at him for another long moment during which he saw something in her expression he couldn't quite identify. Disapproval? A quick intake of breath, and the look disappeared to be replaced with blankness. He thought he might prefer the disapproval, even though it made him curious as hell. He filed that alongside his initial impression of Colby. Interesting.

"Congratulations, Mr. Wakefield." She started up the steps. "I really have to go now."

Nicholas didn't think there would have been much of anything left in the world that could bother him. For the past nine years, he'd had crazies traipsing through his office, calling him obscenities that would curl most people's hair. Why then was he bothered by this woman's tone?

Maybe because there was judgment in it. And he wanted to know why. "Did I say something to offend you, Mrs. Colby?"

His question stopped her again halfway up the stairs. She turned around, slowly retracing her steps. She glanced quickly over her shoulder at the house. "I don't know what would make you think that."

"Why don't we try this again?" He stuck out his hand. "I'm Nicholas Wakefield."

Reluctantly, she offered her own. "Audrey Colby."

Her voice was Southern-soft at the edges. Even in the shadowed light, her eyes ensnared him. Wounded eyes. As if they held scars that ran deep.

She glanced again at the doorway, then stepped deeper into the darkness close to the rock wall behind them. "All those people…it gets a little close."

He couldn't have said why, other than the fact that she was married to his new firm's biggest client, but he was uneasy being here with her. It had been a long time since he'd felt awkward around a woman. "Yeah," he said finally. "That crowd can get a little—" He broke off, deciding she wasn't the person to whom he should reveal his real feelings about the party.

"Presumptuous?" she finished, surprising him.

He tilted his head to one side. "Your word."

"Yes. My word."

"Good music, though." Jill Scott floated out from the speakers at the back of the house, the band apparently taking a break.

She glanced again in the direction of the door.

He leaned a hip against the wall and folded his arms across his chest. "So. Made any resolutions for the New Year?"

A stretch of silence and then she replied, "Only one."

When she failed to ask the same question of him, he volunteered the information anyway. "I made one or two, despite my cynicism. Think you'll stick with yours?"

She looked back out into the darkness, her face set, unsmiling. "Yes," she said.

A door opened behind them. Laughter flowed out from the party into the night. Audrey took a startled step farther into the shadows.

A man crossed the terrace, stopped by one of the carriage lights and lit a cigarette.

"Are you all right?" Nicholas asked.

"Yes. Thank you. But I have to go," she said.

He couldn't explain the disappointment he felt. There was nothing logical about the instant connection he had with this woman. He knew nothing about her, and yet, inexplicably, he wanted to know everything there was to know.

She stepped around him and ran back up the stairs.

He lifted a hand. "Wait!"

But she kept going. And did not look back.

THE RIDE HOME was silent.

But in the back of the limousine, the air hung thick as a Georgia summer afternoon before a storm. Audrey kept her face averted, staring out the window at the passing night.

How easy it would be just to open the door and throw herself onto the pavement. Coward's way out, though. That would only be ending her own misery.

And if it could have been as simple as that, she might have done so long ago.

But there was Sammy.

When the car glided to a stop at the front of the house, the driver opened the back door. Jonathan slid out and waited for Audrey to follow.

"Good night, Thomas," Jonathan said.

"'Night, Mr. Colby. Mrs. Colby."

"Good night." Audrey headed for the front door without waiting for Jonathan. He was right behind her. She tried to stick her key in the lock, but he jerked it from her hand, stabbing it inside the hole and opening the door with a brutal shove.

Marsha Lynch, the sitter, appeared in the hallway, one hand to her throat. "Oh. Hi, Mr. and Mrs. Colby. I wasn't sure that was you at first."

Audrey forced a smile. "Is everything all right, Marsha?"

"Just fine. He's been asleep for hours."

Jonathan pulled out his wallet, paid the girl, his abrupt "Good night," a clear dismissal.

"Call me anytime," Marsha said, her face stiff with uncertainty. She left then, closing the heavy front door behind her.

Jonathan dropped his keys on the entrance table with a clatter that shook Audrey's nerves and rang out in the otherwise silent house.

"Jonathan, please," she said in a quiet voice. "Sammy's—"

"Sammy!" he exploded. "Can you think about anything besides Sammy?" He said the boy's name with a sneer. He'd always insisted that she call him Samuel. It infuriated him when Audrey slipped and called her son by the name she preferred. Jonathan moved toward the living room, jerking his overcoat off and throwing it across the back of the leather couch.

Audrey stood in the foyer for several seconds, her eyes closed, a knot in her stomach. She headed for the stairs then. This could still be avoided. If she just left him alone, maybe it would blow over. She repeated the same rationalizations she always did, even though these episodes were like a storm moving in from the sea. She could do nothing but wait out its arrival.

"Where do you think you're going?" he said, his voice louder now. If she ran upstairs, he would follow, knock down the door, if necessary. And then Sammy would wake up…

She stopped with one hand on the rail, then turned and made her way back to the living room, each step a force of will.

She paused in the doorway. "Jonathan, let's just go to bed. I'm tired, and—"

"Was your little meeting on the terrace so exhausting?" He stood behind the wet bar, pouring scotch into a glass, his voice eerily calm.

She shook her head. "I don't know what you're talking about."

He took a swallow of the liquor, added another shot from the decanter and crossed the room, the click of his shoes on the wood floor menacing. "I'm not in the mood for games, Audrey."

"I went out for some fresh air. That's all."

"Fresh air," he said, sarcasm tainting the words. "And Webster's new partner just happened to be out there at the same time."

Audrey hesitated, her mind racing for an answer that would defuse the situation. But there was no answer. It wouldn't matter what she said. She tried for a note of reason. "He came outside for a couple of minutes. He introduced himself and told me he would be working with you. That's all."

Jonathan moved closer, his eyes narrowed. "I'm aware of how long you were out there."

She met the hard look in his eyes, defiance flaring inside her. How? The view from Laura's room? She pressed her lips together to keep from asking the questions.

"Why would you think he'd look at you, anyway?" His eyes scanned the length of her body. "I was embarrassed to be seen with you. There wasn't a woman there who didn't look better than you tonight. My wife. When are you ever going to develop any taste? You're not in that backwoods family of yours anymore."

She started to remind him he had picked out her dress, but he grabbed her arm and jerked her to him. Her shoulder wrenched at the socket. She bit back a gasp of pain. "Jonathan, stop!"

"It stops when I say it stops." With the back of his hand, he slapped her across the neck. Pain shot through her left side. Excruciating. Reverberating. She moaned. But before she could right herself, he grabbed her and flung her backward across the couch. She hit the hardwood floor on the other side, her shoulder taking the brunt of her weight. She bit her lip to keep from crying out.

Sammy. Think about Sammy. He was upstairs. *Please don't come down. Please.*

Jonathan was in front of her then, pulling her up and flinging her against the wall behind him. She hit it with the same shoulder. But this time, she couldn't hold back the half-scream of anguish. She slumped to the floor where she put her head between her knees and wrapped her arms tightly around herself, praying for oblivion.

"This wouldn't have to happen if you would just listen to me. How many times have I told you that? And Samuel. He's just like you. Neither of you ever listen to anything I say."

Much to her shame, she was crying now. She'd vowed she wouldn't cry anymore. Crying was weak. Gave him what he wanted.

He kicked her then, a hard fierce punt to her left thigh. She kept her arms wrapped around her knees, her head between her legs, praying for the end of it. *I can live through this. One more time. Oh God, Oh God, Oh God, please make him stop. Please don't make me leave my son alone.*

Pleeeassse.

The word echoed once through her throbbing head, and then nothing.

CHAPTER THREE

THE CONFETTI had barely settled to the floor when Nicholas thanked the Websters for their hospitality and then ducked out.

He waited while the valet got his car, then pulled out of the driveway a little too fast in an attempt to accelerate past his preoccupation with Audrey Colby.

Two miles down West Paces Ferry, he let up on the gas, one elbow on the windowsill. What was it about her that had him so rattled? Her desire to be left alone could not have been more clear. And yet out on that terrace, he hadn't been able to make himself walk away. He still felt as if everything inside him had been altered by the few words of conversation they'd had, shaken up to the point that all the pieces of who he had been didn't fit back in their old places.

It was the look in her eyes. A look he'd seen too many times in the eyes of people who had lost a loved one to a senseless crime. A glimpse into the soul of someone who's been broken.

But Audrey Colby? He didn't think so.

He ran a hand over his face. Told himself to leave it alone.

As of tonight, by his own proclamation, he had started over with a career he could accept. No more crusades. No more families looking to him for justice. No more trying to fix in himself what could never be fixed.

Audrey Colby was married to one of the wealthiest men in Georgia. Probably had a life most women would sign up for in a heartbeat.

His problem? He needed to quit imagining that the whole world needed his help.

He turned into his driveway and hit the remote for the garage door.

Something darted out in front of him, seeking cover under the hedge of boxwoods separating his driveway from his neighbor's.

A light above the garage illuminated the center of the driveway, but the bushes were shadowed, making it difficult to see anything.

He rolled down his window, then cut the engine. A soft whimper drifted from under the boxwoods.

Nicholas got out, walked over to the hedge and dropped to his knees. Two unblinking eyes stared back at him.

Black as the night sky, the dog wasn't wearing a collar. It inched backward, making another whimpering sound.

Nicholas sighed. He just wanted to go to bed. Sleep for at least a dozen hours. He lifted the lower branches of the bush. "Hey," he said. "Are you hurt? Come on out. Let me take a look."

But the dog wasn't budging.

Food. He needed a lure. The only thing he had in the car was chewing gum. He grabbed his keys from the ignition and let himself into the house, heading for the kitchen. It looked like a mini shrine to pizza takeout. Four empty boxes sat on the table. One sink was stacked high with coffee cups.

On Mondays, a cleaning service came in and got rid of the boxes, washed all the cups. It was a little like living in a hotel. A place to eat and sleep. Temporary.

He found a loaf of bread in the pantry and removed a couple of slices from the bag. He went back outside, dropped to his knees again, moisture seeping through his tuxedo pants. He held the bread out, tried some coaxing words. The dog sniffed, but didn't move. Nicholas waved the bread around. No interest. He sat for a minute or so, tried again. Still not budging.

Finally, he stood. What else could he do? Drag the dog out from under the bush? He'd tried. He could go with a clear conscience. "Okay. I give up. I'm going in."

But no sooner had he stepped away than the food won out. The dog crawled forward far enough to reach the bread, and gobbled it up in a single bite.

Medium-sized, it appeared no more than three inches wide at its thickest point. In the light, he could see white markings on its legs and chest. The dog's coat was matted in places, dull by malnutrition or maybe parasites. It looked up at him, instantly shrinking to a crouching position. Nicholas's stomach turned. He dropped to his knees again. "It's not like that. I just wanted to make sure you were all right."

The dog scooted away from him, then jumped up and trotted off toward the street.

Headlights flashed from the intersection at the corner. The dog sent an anxious glance over its shoulder. The car was almost in front of them now. Nicholas sprinted after the dog and lunged. The dog dropped flat, looking as if it wanted to melt into the driveway.

"Hey, it's okay. I just didn't want you to get on the road." He reached out to rub the dog's head. The animal quivered.

A clinic a few miles away stayed open all night. He could drop the dog off there, and they could figure out what to do with it.

He picked the animal up, carried it to the car, placed it in the passenger seat and eased the door closed.

He reached the clinic within five minutes, grateful to see lights on when he pulled into a parking space. He got out and jogged to the front door. A small plaque gave instructions to ring the bell. Someone would be right with him.

Thirty seconds later, a young woman appeared. "May I help you?"

"Yeah. I have a dog outside. It's hurt," he said.

"Do you need help bringing it in?"

"No. I'll be right back." He walked to the car and carefully opened the door. In the front seat, the dog had tucked itself nose to tail. He rubbed its back once, then picked it up as gently as possible. It whimpered again. "Sorry," he said.

The young woman held the door for him and then led him to a waiting area and through a set of double doors into a large examining room. "I'm Dr. Filmore, the vet on call tonight."

"Nicholas Wakefield."

The walls were lined with large cages in which a few dogs were sleeping. A dark-brown cocker spaniel raised its head and whined.

"It's all right, Bo," Dr. Filmore said. "You can go back to sleep. On the table here," she directed to Nicholas.

He placed the dog on the stainless tabletop as gently as he could. "I found it outside my house."

The vet dipped her head, then looked back up. "She."

"What?"

"The dog is a she."

"Oh," Nicholas said, nodding.

"She's starving for one thing." The vet was young, but she spoke to the dog in a soft, reassuring voice and ran her hands over her in a way that suggested she knew what she was doing. "I think her left hind leg is broken. It feels like she has a couple of busted ribs, as well. We'll have to get some radiographs."

"Could she have been hit by a car?"

"Maybe. More likely kicked from the way she's acting," the doctor said, her voice flat as a Kansas plain.

A sick feeling settled in Nicholas's stomach. "You see this often?"

"Too often."

He didn't know what to say. What kind of person would kick a helpless dog? "Doesn't it get to you?" he asked.

She sighed. "Yeah. It does. But the only alternative is to quit."

He'd once said the same thing about his own profession. He admired her dedication. Wished for a moment that the fire of his convictions hadn't burned out.

"So you'll fix her up?"

She nodded. "The best I can. You could wait, or go home, and I'll call you when I know something."

"She's not my dog."

The doctor frowned. "Are you saying you don't want to treat her?"

"No. I mean, yes, treat her. But I can't take her home with me."

The young woman dropped her gaze, then looked back up, her jaw a hard line. "Would you like to treat her first and then call Animal Control?"

He heard the disapproval in her voice, and yet he balked at the implication that he was somehow responsible just because he'd happened across the dog. "I can't have a pet," he said. "I work long hours. I'm not set up for—"

"Leave your information with the receptionist out front," she interrupted, then turned her back to him in dismissal.

Nicholas glanced at the dog. She was stretched out with her head on her paws, eyes closed as if she could shut out everything around her. He swung back through the double doors, filled out the forms at the front desk in handwriting that was barely legible. He couldn't get to his car fast enough.

But once he was there, he stared at the building.
Animal Control.

He slapped a hand against the leather steering
wheel, got out and rang the after-hours bell again.
The receptionist let him in this time and pointed
at the doors leading to the examining room. "Go
right on through."

The vet was still busy working on the dog. She
didn't look up when Nicholas came in. "Yes, Mr.
Wakefield?"

"Call me when she's ready to go."

The young doctor glanced up, her smile instantly removing him from her loser's list. "Did
you leave your number?"

"Yes," he said.

"Have a good night then."

IT WAS AFTER 3:00 a.m. when Ross Webster pulled
on his robe and headed downstairs where he
poured himself a stiff shot of scotch. He tossed
half of it back, coughed a couple of times, then
collapsed onto the closest chair, leaning his head
back and closing his eyes.

He was tired. The kind of tired that didn't go
away after a night's sleep.

His life was making him tired.

Ross was old enough to recognize he'd taken
some of the wrong forks in the road. The choices

he'd made were the kind that turned things around permanently. Once, he had been a different man. Or at least he liked to think so.

He'd started out in the public defender's office, hard as that was to believe now. Like his new partner, Wakefield, he'd had his own ideals. Villains to conquer.

Wakefield still had that light in his eyes. Oh, he was convinced it was gone. Had left the prosecutor's office with his tail tucked between his legs because he'd lost one too many cases to the bad guys.

But what Ross had finally figured out—what Wakefield obviously hadn't—was that being one of the good guys didn't get you anywhere. It had started out innocently enough. A little gray bleeding into the black and white.

And then Jonathan Colby had walked into his office. Showed him how he could have the kind of life he'd always wanted. He'd signed on. Just like that. Too late, he'd realized he'd shackled himself to the devil. If he wanted to go anywhere, he had to take Jonathan with him.

And that meant closing his eyes to things that weren't any of his business. Like Colby's treatment of his wife.

How a man could have such a woman and not treat her like fine crystal was beyond his imagination. Things had gotten bad enough to bring the police into the matter a couple of times. With the help of a detective saving for early retirement, Ross had cleaned those up for Jonathan, and he had not been able to look Audrey in the eyes since.

He took another swig of scotch.

Laura appeared in the doorway, tucked inside a fluffy white robe. Without makeup and her high-end clothes, she looked enough like the little girl she had been not so long ago that he felt an actual pain in his chest for his inability to turn back the clock.

"What are you doing up, Daddy?"

"Couldn't sleep. Still wired from the party, I guess. You?"

She leaned against the doorjamb and folded her arms across her chest, looking as if she had something on her mind.

"What is it, honey?"

She tipped her head, didn't answer for a moment, and then said, "Do you think Jonathan and Audrey are happy?"

The question took him by surprise. "As happy as anyone, I guess. Why do you ask?"

"I don't know. They don't look happy."

"That's their business then, don't you think?"

She shrugged. "I just wonder why people stay together if they're not happy being with each other."

"Human nature, I guess," he said. "Hard to get

off the train once it's headed down the tracks." He thought of his own marriage, his clear understanding of why Sylvia had stayed with him all these years. Nice enough meal ticket for a girl from rural Georgia. If he'd once thought it had to do with anything other than that, he'd been permanently cured of his disillusion.

"That's a pretty dismal outlook. I don't think people should stay together if it's not working."

"Probably not," he conceded, too weary to argue.

"So why do you?"

He met her gaze, started to pretend he didn't know what she meant, then surprised himself by saying, "Your mom and I have been together a long time."

"So that's a reason?"

"One."

"How about another?"

"Something about age, I think. Things you couldn't have imagined yourself doing, standing for, when you were younger just don't really seem worth the battle."

"Now there's a life goal. Settling. You know, Daddy, I'm not subscribing."

Ross heard the disapproval in his daughter's voice. On the day she'd been born, his biggest hope was that she would grow up to be proud of him. There was something infinitely deflating in the realization that your child did not respect you. "Maybe your life will be completely different."

A smile touched her mouth. "If I have any say in it."

Her certainty was hard to refute. And he hoped she would be right.

"I'm headed to the kitchen," she said, her tone lighter, as if she had decided to give him a reprieve. "Want something warm to drink?"

"Sure, honey," he said. "Thanks."

"Be right back."

He watched her leave the room. Even her walk was marked with confidence. In Laura's eyes, the world was hers for the taking. He had spoiled his daughter. That, Ross could not deny. But he loved her.

He wondered if Audrey Colby had a father who felt the same about her.

He could only imagine what he would do if Laura ever got involved with a man who mistreated her. Something in his gut tightened, needle-sharp. Laura might be spoiled, but she was the one good thing he'd done in his life. He'd die before she'd end up like Audrey.

He was sorry for her. Really, he was. But he wasn't a white-hat guy.

He couldn't save her.

Hell, he'd be lucky if he saved himself.

AUDREY AWOKE to a pain so intense it took her a moment to figure out what it was. Maybe she'd died. Maybe this was what death felt like when you'd failed to live your life to expectation.

She opened her eyes and stared at the ceiling. The room was nearly dark, the only light shining through from the kitchen. She tried to sit up. Something sharp stabbed her palm. Wincing, she yanked her hand away, blood trickling down her wrist. Shards of glass, the remains of a broken table lamp, lay around her, the shade resting on its side like an old hat someone had thrown away.

Moaning, she straightened and leaned back against the wall, fighting the wave of nausea threatening to overcome her. She touched her hand to her throbbing shoulder, then tried to move it. White-hot pain shot through her arm. She dropped her head back and wondered how many days she would have to hide from the world to cover this one up. Thank God it was winter. Thank God for turtlenecks and gloves.

She squeezed her eyes shut, wiping at the tears sliding down one cheek with the back of her hand. She despised herself for the tears. Tears were useless, would get her nowhere. They were weak and powerless and self-pitying. The last person she felt sorry for was herself.

She'd long since ceased to think of the poor excuse of a woman that she had become as someone she knew. The woman who now sat huddled on her living-room floor was a stranger. Someone she did not know, resembling in no way the woman Audrey had once thought she would become. This woman was a victim. Weak. Despicable.

Why hadn't she walked away as soon as she'd seen Nicholas Wakefield standing on that terrace?

Maybe because he'd been a stranger, and there was anonymity in that, someone with no pre-drawn conclusions about her. At the party, she'd barely spoken to anyone, knowing that to linger too long would be to arouse Jonathan's anger. Outside, in the darkness, some almost-forgotten part of her had been hungry for a few moments of uncensored conversation with another human be-ing. A human being who knew nothing about her life, who might think she was as normal as the rest of the world.

"Mama?"

Audrey jerked up. Her nine-year-old son stood in the doorway, his face white with fear. Audrey glanced at the mess around her, the shattered lamp, the overturned coffee table, realizing what she must look like. "Oh, Sammy. It's okay. Stay right there."

Taking a deep breath, she slid across the floor, her back to the wall, each move agonizing. She hadn't made it to the doorway before he launched himself at her, flinging his arms around her neck and gripping her as if he were about to drown. She winced at the spasm of pain that racked through her, but pulled him close and held him tight.

Sammy cried quietly, his chest shaking. She closed her eyes and pressed his face to her shoulder, soothing him with her voice and her hands.

"I thought you were dead," he finally managed to say. "I saw you against the wall, and I thought—"

Audrey's eyes welled with tears. "It's okay, sweetie. I'm all right. Shh."

"Why does he hurt you, Mommy?" Sammy asked, his voice breaking at the end.

Audrey drew back and brushed his hair away from his face, gently rubbing the tears from his cheek with her thumb. "Sammy, I'm sorry. I'm so sorry."

Her son, her precious son, looked up at her with fear and anguish in his eyes. For that, Audrey hated herself most of all.

Despite the pain grabbing at her, she walked with him up the stairs, her arm around his shoulders, tucking him to her side.

In his room, she helped him into bed, smoothing a hand over his fine hair. Sitting there beside the son she loved more than she would ever have believed it possible to love, Audrey thought of what a different life she had once imagined for herself, for the children she might have. How had things turned out this way?

The truth? She had never seen it coming.

CHAPTER FOUR

As a SENIOR in high school, Audrey took a job with the Colbys, the most affluent family in Lanier, Georgia. They could trace their bloodlines to the earliest records in the courthouse, and Martha Colby took great pride in running her home in much the same way her husband's ancestors had. Even though Audrey had originally been hired to work two evenings a week and every Saturday, her hours had continued to increase when one of the housekeepers had to leave.

Audrey didn't mind working extra. While she liked her actual classes, she didn't enjoy the social aspects of school. Up until junior high, she had liked everything about it and had looked forward to running track.

But then her body had started to change, and along with it, the rest of her life as well. In her freshman year, her bra size went from 34 A to 36 C. At five-three, Audrey was small-framed, petite even, and the change was more than noticeable. Suddenly, boys treated her differently. She hated the look in their eyes, detested the snickers that followed her down the hall. But worst of all were the nicknames she heard bandied about behind her back, the suggestive remarks the boys made when she walked by. One day, she'd gone into biology class and found one of those nicknames carved into the top of the desk.

She'd left the class and called her mom to come and get her, claiming she had a stomachache. She'd spent the rest of the afternoon curled up on her bed, humiliated.

Her mother came into her room, smoothing a hand over her hair. "What is it, honey? What's wrong?"

Audrey turned over, unwelcome tears welling in her eyes. "I hate school, Mama. I don't want to go back."

"It's the changes in your body," her mother said softly. "Am I right?"

Audrey bit her lip, before admitting in a low voice, "It's awful."

Sarah Williams took her daughter's hand and squeezed it between both of hers. "Oh, baby, you've just matured faster than some girls. Do you know how many women would love to have your figure?"

"I'm not a woman. And the boys make fun of me."

Her mother pressed her lips together. "That's because they're immature and don't know any better."

"Please don't make me go back."

"Audrey." Her mother's voice held a note of wistfulness as if she wished she could snap her fingers and take the pain away. But she couldn't. And they both knew it. "It won't last forever, honey. The older you get, the better things will be. I promise."

In a way, she was right. Audrey wore clothing that helped to conceal her figure, loose-fitting blouses and jumpers. She never wore sweaters or anything that remotely emphasized her breasts. The nicknames ceased. At least where she could hear them. But the boys were still interested in one thing. And after a few dates that resulted in little more than fumbling and groping, she decided dating wasn't for her.

Instead, she threw herself into her schoolwork and had so far maintained the highest GPA in her class. She spent her free time painting—mostly portraits, scenes from small-town life. She loved the mystery of a blank canvas, starting out with nothing but white space and capturing a moment of time there.

Halfway through her senior year she went to work for the Colbys, and although she got a little less sleep than before, it was worth it to have the extra money. She'd recently been accepted at

Georgia State. Going to college was important to her. No one else in her family had ever been. Her mother and father were counting on her to be the first. Money was tight, though. Her father had worked in a lumber mill for the past twenty years, and her mother took in sewing and alterations in addition to her job at the local Rexall. Audrey wanted to help with her tuition so she took as many extra hours as she could.

One afternoon, Mrs. Colby asked her to dust in the library. With its walnut-paneled walls and inviting reading lamps, it was a room she could have spent weeks in without ever leaving. She wiped each of the frames positioned on the round tables, handling them with care. An eight-by-ten photo in a pewter frame caught her eye. A young man with glossy black hair and smooth, dark skin, smiled up at her, his eyes hinting at self-assurance. The Colbys' only son, Jonathan. She'd heard of him through her older brother. Jonathan Colby was a local icon of sorts, the rich kid who went to boarding school and moved away after college.

Audrey rubbed at the glass on the photograph, then placed it back on the table. But her gaze lingered on his handsome face, and she wondered if he ever came home.

After that day, she found herself thinking about him. In school while the teacher was lecturing. At night when she turned off her lamp and lay in bed. She wondered what it would be like to go out with someone older and more mature, unlike the boys in school.

Jonathan Colby remained snagged in her thoughts, even though she'd never met him, even though he was older by ten years or so.

But on the following Tuesday, she forgot all of her arguments about putting him from her mind. She was in the kitchen helping Mary, an older woman who had been with the Colbys for years as a housekeeper. Mary touched a hand to the grey braid wound into a coil at the nape of her neck. "We'll have to get the house extra clean this week," Mary said. "Mrs. Colby says Jonathan is coming home over the weekend. She's having a dinner on Saturday night for him. She asked me to check with you about working late."

The dish in Audrey's hand clattered to the floor. "I'm sorry," she said, bending over to pick it up, grateful that it hadn't broken. "I'll be glad to."

Mary sent her a knowing look and then said with a chuckle, "Jonathan always did have that effect on the girls."

It was the slowest week of Audrey's life. She thought the weekend would never arrive. On Saturday afternoon, she took extra care getting ready. Standing back and looking at herself in the mirror, she decided that she looked older, a little more sophisticated.

Once she arrived at the Colby house, Audrey was a batch of nerves, her stomach tightening every time the kitchen door swung open.

When it was time to serve dessert, Audrey followed Mary into the dining room where the din of conversation rose and fell around the twelve-person table.

She kept her eyes on the serving cart, too nervous to look up.

"Could you put one of these in each bowl, Audrey?" Mary asked, handing her some silver spoons.

"Sure," she said, glancing at the head of the table and spotting him for the first time. To his right sat a dark-haired girl laughing at something he'd just said close to her ear. Audrey couldn't look away from the two of them. He was every bit as handsome as his photo. More so. And the girl beside him was tall and striking in an off-the-shoulder black cocktail dress.

Audrey started to turn, but he glanced up just then and caught her gaze. Her cheeks went warm, the blush spreading across her whole body. He didn't look away for several long seconds, and she could have sworn she saw a flicker of interest in his laughing blue eyes.

She moved toward his end of the table and

placed the spoons in each bowl, feeling his eyes upon her still. Gripped with shyness, she could not bring herself to glance up again.

A few minutes later, she escaped to the kitchen. Once there, she wet a paper towel with cool water and pressed it to her cheeks. She'd spent the week fantasizing about a guy she'd never met, had only seen a picture of. And now that she'd seen him in real life, with an infatuated girl beside him, she felt… What? Disappointed. The ridiculousness of the admission did not escape her.

Mary returned to the kitchen a few minutes later. "So what did you think?"

"Of what?" she asked, continuing to scrub the pot in the sink without looking up.

"Young Jonathan, of course."

"Oh. He's very handsome."

"And as usual, he's got a new young lady with him tonight." Mary shook her head. "I don't think he'll ever settle down. He's too busy sampling."

It was after 1:00 a.m. by the time the two of them had everything washed and put back in place.

"That should about do it," Mary said, wiping her hands on her apron. "You go on home now. Will you be all right by yourself?"

"I'll be fine," Audrey reassured her.

"See you at eleven tomorrow?"

"Okay," she said, letting herself out the kitchen

door. Getting in her mother's old green Falcon, she turned the key in the ignition. An awful grinding noise rang out like gunshots in the quiet neighborhood.

She tried it again, but this time the noise was worse. A knock sounded at the window. Audrey jumped, one hand to her throat. Jonathan peered down at her, smiling. Her heart started pounding in her ears.

"Mind if I give it a try?" she heard him ask through the closed window.

This wasn't exactly how she'd envisioned the two of them meeting. But grateful for his help, she nodded and got out. He slid behind the wheel. When the same thing happened after two tries, he said, "I don't think it's going anywhere tonight."

"I think you're right," she said, forcing herself to meet his gaze. His face had relaxed into a kind smile, and she noticed that he had a smudge of red lipstick on his collar. Apparently, he'd just gotten back from taking his date home.

"I don't think we got properly introduced," he said. "I'm Jonathan Colby."

"Audrey Williams."

He looked at her and said, "Audrey. I'll be glad to give you a lift. You can leave the car here tonight."

Something inside her thrilled at the thought.

But she didn't want him to feel obligated to take her. "I can call a cab."

"It's not a problem."

She hesitated, before saying, "If you're sure you won't mind."

"Not at all." He smiled at her then, looking exactly like the man in the photograph she'd been fantasizing about all week.

AUDREY'S HOUSE was approximately twenty-five minutes away, on the other side of town. For once, she was glad of the distance. Sitting in Jonathan Colby's BMW with late-night radio playing in the background was like something she might have dreamed. The tan leather seat felt like butter against her skin, and he had the sunroof open, leaving a square of stars visible above them.

"How long have you been working for my parents?" he asked as they backed out of the driveway and then sped down the tree-lined street.

"A few months."

"I thought you must have started since the last time I was home. I would have remembered you."

The words made her heart beat a little faster. It would be foolish to read anything into them, but his smile made her think he'd meant them as a compliment. "Your mother's very nice," she said, looking down at her lap.

"Yes, she is," he agreed, the smile suddenly disappearing. "Are you in college?"

"I'm a senior. In high school," she said, flattered.

He slowed for a stop sign, one hand on the steering wheel, the other on the gear shift. "You could have fooled me."

Again, the remark found its spot in her heart, and she smiled at him. "You live in Atlanta, don't you?"

He nodded. "I'm running an arm of Dad's business there."

"Do you like it? Atlanta, I mean."

"Yeah. It's a great town. There's a lot to do."

She didn't want to tell him that she'd never been even though it was only four hours away. Her family hadn't traveled much. Neither of her parents liked to stray too far from home.

They chatted for the duration of the drive to her house. She told him where to turn when they reached her street. He stopped in front of the driveway, flicking the car lights off.

"Thank you so much for the ride," she said.

"You're welcome."

Audrey wished for a reason to linger. None of the guys she'd dated came close to this dark-haired, confident man.

"You have a boyfriend, Audrey?" he asked.

"No one special."

"That's surprising."

She shrugged. "I'm going to college next year. And I work part-time. There's not much room for anything else."

"You're smart to keep it that way for now."

In that moment, Audrey was glad there was no one else. She sensed that if she shifted in his direction, he would have kissed her. But she didn't have the courage to try it.

Unnerved by the awareness between them, she looked down at her lap and said, "Thank you for the ride, Jonathan. I really appreciate it."

He put a hand on the steering wheel, and said, "No problem."

"I'll get my dad to come over in the morning and take a look at the car."

"Will you be coming with him?"

She nodded. "I have to be there for work at eleven."

"Good. Then I guess I'll see you at lunch?"

She smiled. "I guess so."

THE NEXT MORNING, Audrey's father drove her to work and called a tow truck for her mother's car. The Colbys came in from church just before twelve-thirty. Audrey's stomach fluttered at the sound of their voices in the foyer. She could hear Jonathan's low tones and felt a fresh rush of anticipation at the thought of seeing him again.

She followed Mary into the dining room, carrying steaming bowls of mashed potatoes and cream-style corn. Her gaze immediately found him, seated again at the far end of the table. The same dark-haired young woman sat next to him. Audrey's heart dropped to the floor.

She tried not to look at him again and went about the business of putting food on the table, wanting only to finish so she could escape back to the kitchen. Once there, she ran her hand under the cool tap water and splashed a little on her face.

It was after three o'clock when the kitchen door swung open. She looked up from wiping the counters. Jonathan stood in the doorway, and she could not deny the gladness she felt at the sight of him. "Hi."

He smiled at her. "Did you get your car fixed?"

She shook her head. "Dad had a tow truck pick it up."

"Will you need a ride home then?"

"I'll call him when I'm through here."

"I'll be glad to take you. I'll be on my way out of town anyway. I'm heading back to Atlanta in a little while."

Audrey hesitated, recalling Mary's earlier warning. But even though she knew the woman was probably right, she found herself saying, "If you're sure it won't be too much trouble."

"No trouble at all. I'll go upstairs and pack up the rest of my things. How much longer will you be?"

"Twenty minutes or so?"

"I'll meet you back here."

Audrey called her mom and told her she had a ride home.

Jonathan was back in exactly twenty minutes. "I already said goodbye to my folks, so if you're ready—"

"All set." She reached for her sweater where she'd hung it earlier on the hook behind the door.

"Here, let me help." He took the sweater and held it for her while she shrugged her arms inside. His hands grazed the side of her shoulders, sending unexpected sparks of electricity through her.

"Thank you," she said, not meeting his gaze for fear that he would see awareness in her eyes.

"Do you have to be home right away?" he asked, once they were in the car.

The question surprised her. "Not right away."

"Want to take a walk in the park?"

"Sure. I'd love to."

He pulled over at a 7-Eleven, coming out a couple of minutes later with two Cokes and a bag of chips. "Not much of a picnic," he said, "but it's the best I can do on short notice."

She laughed, thinking it was wonderful that he'd thought of it at all.

They parked on the street beside the entrance. Jonathan opened her door for her and pulled a blanket from the trunk. By the pond, Jonathan spread out the quilt, tossed the chips and Cokes in one corner and motioned for her to sit. She did, pulling her knees up in front of her chest.

He sat down beside her, plucked a blade of grass and twirled it between his fingers. "Why do you do that?"

"What?"

"Hide yourself."

She avoided his eyes. "I don't know what you mean."

"The clothes you wear. The way you hunch your shoulders. The way you're hiding behind your knees right now."

Face hot, she kept her gaze on the grass in front of the quilt.

"You're beautiful, Audrey," he said. "There's nothing to be ashamed of in that."

They stayed for a good two hours, talking about his work, her hopes for the future. Despite their age difference, they shared many of the same interests, good books, art.

He didn't kiss her that day, but she knew in her heart that he wanted to. He took her home a little before six, and she hated for the day to end, knowing she'd probably never see him again.

"Thank you, Jonathan," she said when he stopped in her driveway. "For the ride. And the afternoon."

"You're welcome," he said, watching her with considering eyes. He reached inside his jacket and pulled out his wallet. Handing her a business card, he said, "If you ever need anything—"

"Thanks. Have a good trip back." She got out of the car and ran up the walk to her house.

FOR THE NEXT WEEK, she looked at the card every night before she went to bed. She debated about writing to him, talking herself out of it at least five times before deciding there wouldn't be anything wrong with a thank-you note.

She went to the drugstore and bought a pack of stationery cards with a pond on the front and ducks standing by the water's edge. She kept the note brief.

> Dear Jonathan,
> I just wanted to thank you again for taking me home last Saturday night and for the picnic on Sunday. I really enjoyed our conversation.
> Audrey Williams

She agonized over sending it, but finally forced herself to put it in the mailbox and push it from her mind.

Four days later, she heard back from him.

Audrey,

I'm coming home next weekend. If you don't have to work Saturday night, I'd love to take you out for dinner. If you'd like to go, give me a call at the number on the card I gave you.

Jonathan

Audrey reread the note three times before letting herself believe it was true.

She ran to her room and pulled the card out of her jewelry box where she'd hidden it. She went downstairs to the phone in the kitchen and dialed the number.

THAT AFTERNOON, she went into the den where Mrs. Colby was having tea and knocked at the door. "Excuse me, Mrs. Colby?"

"Yes, Audrey?"

"May I speak with you for a moment?"

"Of course. Come in." She put down her cup and motioned for Audrey to sit opposite her on the sofa. "What is it, dear?"

"I wondered if I might have next Saturday night off."

Mrs. Colby smiled. "A young man, I presume? As pretty as you are, I'm surprised you don't need every Saturday night off. Of course you may."

"Thank you, Mrs. Colby," Audrey said, smiling in relief. She wondered what the woman would think if she knew Audrey was having dinner with her son and felt a stab of guilt for not telling her. But maybe that was Jonathan's place.

Mrs. Colby reached for the teapot, refilling her cup. "You're welcome, dear. You've done an awfully good job for us. I hope you know we appreciate it." She leaned forward to put the pot back on its tray. The neckline of her dress slipped aside, revealing an almost blackish bruise on her left shoulder. It was horrible looking, the worst bruise Audrey had ever seen.

"Mrs. Colby," she said, before she could stop herself. "What happened?"

The older woman jumped, her cup clattering in its saucer. With her free hand, she hastily pulled the dress back in place, her expression closing like a door to a storm wind. "I slipped on the terrace steps the other day and landed on my shoulder. I'm afraid it left an awful bruise."

"Oh," Audrey said. "Are you all right?"

"Fine, dear. I've had worse falls than that," she said. "Now, if that's all, I'm sure Mary is wondering where you are."

"Yes, ma'am," Audrey said, then went back to the kitchen. She didn't think about the incident anymore until that night after she'd gone to bed.

There was no reason not to believe Mrs. Colby. But something about the way she'd acted hadn't felt right, as if she were trying to hide something. She thought of Mr. Colby, the few times she'd passed him in the house, his face stormy, as if he were always angry about something.

For a moment, just a brief moment, Audrey wondered about their relationship, and whether Mr. Colby had anything to do with the bruise on his wife's shoulder.

But that was crazy. Jon Colby was a highly respected member of the community. And Mrs. Colby didn't seem like the kind of woman to put up with something like that.

Audrey put the questions from her mind and focused on her upcoming dinner with Jonathan.

It was a mistake she would live to regret.

CHAPTER FIVE

SAMMY WAITED until his mother had left the room and closed the door before he opened his eyes. She'd sat there a long time, not saying anything, just brushing her hand back and forth across his hair.

He'd kept his eyes shut so she would think he was asleep. If he'd opened them, he'd have started crying like a baby again. He didn't want her to see him crying. And besides that, he couldn't look at the ugly purple bruises on her neck. His mommy had the prettiest face in the world, and he hated his dad for hitting her.

Beneath the covers, he pressed his palms together, the tips of his fingers touching his chin. Squeezing his eyes shut, he whispered into the darkness the words she had taught him when he was little. He usually asked God to watch over his grandma and grandpa Williams. And sometimes he wished for a brother or sister so that when he felt scared they could huddle in the dark together instead of just him here alone. But then he always felt guilty for that part because he didn't want a little brother or sister who had to be scared all the time.

Tonight he didn't ask for either of those things. "Dear God, please take care of Mama. Don't let Daddy hurt her anymore. Please make me strong so I can take care of her. Please make it fast, too, because I'm afraid he'll hurt her really bad soon. Please, God. Amen."

Sammy turned his face into the pillow and pulled his knees up against his chest. He didn't want to cry. He'd asked God to make him strong. But the tears came anyway because it would be a very long time before he would be big enough to take care of her.

ON NEW YEAR'S DAY, Nicholas drove to PetsMart and spent an amazing $477 on dog stuff.

Collar. Leash. Food and water bowls. Dry food. Canned food. Bed. Various and assorted forms of entertainment: chew toys, tennis balls, Frisbees.

A friendly woman from the clinic had called mid-morning to say his dog was ready to be picked up. Nicholas had spent his entire adult life avoiding commitment of any kind. Commitment meant being responsible for something or someone. And failure to meet expectation inevitably meant letting that something or someone down. A long time ago, he'd vowed never to put himself in that position again.

And to date, he hadn't.

Yet here he was.

His dog.

He sat in the waiting room for a half hour before a young man in a white lab coat walked out.

"Hello," he said, sticking out his hand. "I'm Dr. Earnest. Dr. Filmore brought me up to date on everything she did for—" He glanced at the chart. "Does she have a name?"

"No."

"Your dog. Anyway, the left hind leg did show a fracture. Ribs were okay. Just bruised. The more immediate concern seems to be the fact that she won't eat or drink. We've given her some fluids and had her out of the crate trying to cheer her up a bit this morning, but she's having none of it."

"What do you suggest?"

"Patience, I guess." He sighed. "Sometimes it takes a very long time for animals who've been where this one has probably been to trust again. If ever."

Suddenly awash in doubt about what he was taking on, Nicholas said, "Maybe I should leave her here for a few days."

"This is an emergency clinic only. I'm afraid we're not set up for that. You can pay up front, and I'll bring her out."

Nicholas did as requested, and within two minutes, Dr. Earnest pushed back through the swinging door. Two feet behind him was the dog Nicholas had come to pick up, following on a blue nylon leash. His heart dropped. The dog hunkered as close to the floor as was possible in a splint, her tail tucked between her legs, ears pressed flat.

Dr. Earnest handed Nicholas the leash. "Good luck. I'd take her in to your regular vet in about a week to have the leg checked."

"Thanks."

"Don't expect an overnight miracle. My guess is she had it pretty rough."

Nicholas looked into the dog's wary eyes. "Yeah," he said. "I suspect she did."

AUDREY SAT at the kitchen table, sipping from a nearly full cup of lukewarm coffee. It had no taste this morning, no appeal. Through the window, she watched Sammy climb a tree in the backyard, his skinny arms pulling him from limb to limb until he reached the tree house where he spent far too much of his time. But then, how could she protest when she understood why he would rather be there than in this house?

Footsteps sounded in the hallway. Her stomach fluttered. She gripped the handle of her coffee cup, forcing her gaze to the newspaper in front of her.

Jonathan pulled a glass from the cabinet and sat down across from her. He poured himself some juice, then reached for a section of the paper. Still, she did not look at him.

"Are you okay?" he asked, his voice neutral, as if he were asking whether the forecast predicted rain today.

"Fine," she said, equally neutral. This was the way it went. Cautious concern the next day. Let's get things back to normal. She stood, wincing at the soreness in her ribs. She pressed her lips together and walked to the sink where she rinsed out her coffee cup.

Jonathan flipped through the paper, finally slapping it closed and abruptly pushing his chair back from the table.

"Let's not do the silent treatment, okay?" he said, irritation underscoring the words. "I'm sorry for what happened last night."

Anchoring her hands to the sink, she closed her eyes, fighting back a wave of fury so intense she thought she might actually drown beneath it. *Sorry.* And that fixed it. *Sorry* always fixed it. "I don't want to talk about it," she said, her voice barely audible.

He crossed the floor, put a hand on her shoulder and turned her to face him. "Let's just get past it, okay?"

She made herself look at him, saw the reprimand in his eyes, and for the life of her, could barely hold back the scream erupting inside her.

He glanced away, dropping his hand. "You know, none of this would ever happen if you didn't always find a way to push my buttons."

The audacity of the statement unraveled whatever threads of control she'd managed to stitch together throughout a sleepless night. Her fault. Always, it was her fault.

She gripped the edge of the kitchen counter. Stay calm. She had a plan to carry out. There was too much to risk now by saying anything at all. "Forget it, all right?" she said softly.

"I think that would be best," he said, lifting her chin with his hand. "Samuel. He'll like the school, you know. You'll see that I'm right about it."

Audrey stiffened, forcing herself to say, "Maybe so."

"When I was his age, I would have given anything to get out of my house," he said, his voice distant with memory. "Going away to school was the greatest thing that ever happened to me."

"Why?" she asked, unable to stop herself. "Because your father treated your mother the way you treat me?"

Surprise widened his eyes. A shadow passed across his face. He stared at her for a moment, and then said, "That was different. I'm not like my father. He was—"

"What, Jonathan?" she asked quickly. It was the first time he'd ever made any allusion to the situation he'd grown up in, a situation that to Audrey's knowledge continued to this day. For years, Jonathan had made excuses as to why they couldn't go home to Lanier for a visit, but on the rare occasions when his parents came to Atlanta, Audrey saw the two of them through different eyes from those of the naive girl she had been when she'd worked in the Colby home. And even though there was no answer that could change this existence masquerading as a life between them, she needed to hear one.

But he stepped away, walked back to the table and picked up his glass. "Different." he said again. He reached for the paper, tucked it under one arm and set his glass in the sink. "I'm going in to the office. I'll be back later."

For a long time after he'd gone, Audrey stood in the exact same spot. And then she made herself move, stacking dishes in the dishwasher, wiping off the counter, putting away Sammy's cereal, each task a link in the seconds, minutes, hours that would lead to tomorrow and the step she would take to change her life, her son's life.

THE DAY AFTER New Year's, Audrey drove to the library. Sammy didn't have school and was happy to go with her. It was one of his favorite things to do. During the short drive, he said little, but stared out the window most of the way. The look on his face made her heart ache with love and sympathy. She wanted to reassure him, tell him everything would be okay, that this time, she would make certain.

The Buckhead Trace-Matherson Library was a brick three-story structure with tall-paned windows and an arched doorway. An enormous piece of modern art sat at its entrance. Audrey walked Sammy through the double doors and to the children's section on the first floor. "You'll be okay?" she asked, smoothing a hand across his blond hair.

"Yeah," he said. "It's like being left at Disneyland."

Sammy loved to read, but rarely did so at home to avoid his father's ridicule for being a bookworm instead of getting outside and playing ball like other boys. Just the thought sent a fresh twist of resentment through Audrey. She told her son she would be back in a little while and headed for the elevator.

There were several computers set up on the second floor. The stations were all empty, and Audrey sat down in front of one, thankful that no one was here today.

She put one hand on the keyboard, anxiety making her nearly lightheaded. She blinked it away, logged onto the account she had set up under a fake name, clicked on Write Mail and typed in the address she had memorized. Several minutes passed before she could bring herself to type the words. Doing so felt like jumping off a cliff, with no guarantee of ever hitting bottom.

Hello. I am told you might be able to help me.

She sat for a moment, her mind blank. How to say in a few words what her life had become? She wanted to make her case without going into any more detail than necessary. Somehow, writing it down for another human being to see left her feeling scalded with shame.

She put her fingers on the keyboard again, her hands shaking.

I am in an abusive marriage. I have made other attempts to get out of the situation. Each of them failed. I want to leave the country with my son February 7th. Please. Can you help me?

Footsteps sounded on the tile floor. She glanced over her shoulder, terror tripping through her. She hit Send and exited the screen.

A janitor emptied a small trash can at the station next to her, then walked on.

One hand to her heart, Audrey looked back at the computer. A message popped up.

Your mail has been sent.

She stared at the words. Too late to take it back now. Somewhere out there, another individual would receive her e-mail, read it and judge whether or not she deserved to be helped.

She thought about the kind-eyed nurse she'd met during her last trip to the emergency room. The young woman had slipped inside Audrey's cubicle, pulling the curtain closed, her gaze knowing, sympathetic.

"Here," she had said, pressing a small piece of paper into Audrey's hand, her voice little more than a whisper. "I've been where you are. If you need a way out, use this address."

"What is it?" Audrey asked.

"It will connect you with a group of people who help women like you and me make a new life in another place."

Audrey studied the woman, not sure what to say. "Did you—?"

"Yes," she said quietly. "For five years. My

daughters and I. My husband was killed two years ago. We don't have to hide anymore."

Audrey heard the relief behind the woman's words, and yet at the same time, saw the conflicting emotions of pain and regret in her eyes. "I'm sorry," she said.

The nurse shook her head. "For me, there would have been no possibility of a happy ending if he had found me. You know where you are. If you take this step, make sure you're ready. It will be permanent."

That had been three months ago. Since then Audrey had been preparing for this day. Saving money. Obtaining passports for Sammy and herself.

During the course of their marriage, Audrey had made three attempts to leave Jonathan. Each time she had believed she would never go back.

The first time she'd packed up her things and driven home to Lanier. Jonathan had waited until her mother and father left the house one morning before pulling into the driveway and knocking at the door.

He'd appealed to her at first with soft words and apologies. "Audrey, I'm sorry. I didn't mean it. I know you're upset. I'll make it up to you."

"Go away, Jonathan. I don't want to see you," she'd said from behind the closed door.

"This is crazy. Open up. I need to talk to you."

She stood at the door, arms folded across her

chest, trying to control her shaking. "Just leave, Jonathan. Please."

He didn't say anything for a few moments, but when he spoke again, she heard the edge of rage in his voice. "Open the door, Audrey, or I'll open it myself."

The seconds ticked by while she stood there, her forehead pressed against the door, her eyes closed. She just wanted it to end. Wanted him to leave her alone, let her go on with her life.

"Unless you want the whole neighborhood to know I'm here, open the door. Now."

There was no mistaking the threat behind the words, and she'd finally opened it. Sammy was out back playing. She didn't want him to know Jonathan was here. She just wanted this to end peacefully. She wanted to be left alone. That was all. Just left alone.

Jonathan came inside, his face set. "Come home, Audrey. This is insane."

She stared up at him, wondering how he could say that with a straight face. "Insane is what goes on in our house."

"I told you I was sorry," he said, sounding frighteningly reasonable. "What else can I do?"

"I'm not asking you to do anything. Except go."

He moved farther into the living room, looking out the picture window to Sammy, playing on the swingset. He looked back at her then. "You don't really think I'd let you keep him, do you?"

The words sliced through her like a knife, cold and cutting. "This isn't the time to talk about this," she said carefully.

"When would be a better time?" he asked, the words deceptively soft.

"Jonathan—"

"I advise you to come home, Audrey. If you don't, I will guarantee you don't stand a chance in hell of getting custody. You have no job. No education. No money of your own. Nothing—"

"Except the fact that I'll tell any judge who'll listen what you've been doing to me," she said, hot anger rearing inside her.

"What *I've* been doing?" He laughed. "Don't you mean what we've been doing? Fighting occasionally like any normal couple?"

She stared at him in disbelief. He was serious. "A normal couple? You think that's what we are?"

"We wouldn't have any problems, Audrey, if you would just remember that I don't like my wife flirting with every man she meets."

The accusation was so unjust, so unfair, that she felt as if she'd been punched in the stomach. It wasn't so much the accusation itself, but the realization that he believed it to be true. Could he make someone else believe it? A judge? She glanced out the window at Sammy, and a chill ran through her. No one knew better than she did how persuasive and convincing Jonathan could be. When he wanted something, nothing would stop him until he got it.

And so she had gone back, the walls of the prison in which she lived pressing ever closer, Jonathan's need to control her reaching new levels. He cut off all access to cash, allowing her to carry department-store credit cards and a gas card only.

The computer beeped, bringing her thoughts to the present. A box popped up on the screen.

You have mail.

Heart pounding, Audrey clicked on New Mail.

Dear Audrey,

We are an underground network of volunteers united in an effort to support women and children living in abusive situations.

This address could only have been given to you by someone within our organization. For that person to have done so, he or she has witnessed evidence that you need our assistance.

Our network of volunteers—across this country, and other countries, as well—is made up of ordinary citizens: teachers, nurses, lawyers, doctors who believe that many abusive relationships will never be resolved, but will most likely end in the death of the victimized spouse and/or her children.

The statistics support this belief.

Our goal is to put you in a situation where you can start a new life. Any contact you have with anyone from your current life will jeopardize your safety. Please be certain you are ready to resort to these measures.

You and your son will need passports.

I will contact you at this address when I have a location for you. Please check daily. I am sure you know the seriousness of this matter. In taking your son out of the country without your husband's permission, you may be charged with kidnapping should he ever find you.

If this is what you feel you must do, I do not wish to discourage you. At the same time, we must be certain you are completely aware of what you are doing.

May God Bless You,
Kathryn Milborn

Audrey sat for a moment, stunned by the stark warning. And yet, she had known there would be no turning back once she'd taken this step. But what choice did she have? To stay was to ensure one eventual outcome. She could no longer tell herself that things would get better. Jonathan's rage continued to escalate, each incident stoking the fire of the next.

She had to get out. This time for good. If not for herself, then for Sammy.

She reached for the mouse and clicked on Reply.

THE FIRST FEW DAYS at Webster & Associates weren't exactly what Nicholas had expected.

He kept waiting for the excitement to kick in, for the adrenaline that had gotten him through every day as a prosecutor to start pumping.

But there wasn't much in the stacks of files now occupying his desk that incited either excitement or adrenaline. Bureaucracy and red tape appeared to be the name of the game.

His office was everything a corporate attorney's office should be. Soft leather couches adjacent to his desk. Original artwork on the walls. None of which was his taste, but was meant to impress, to say, "Trust us. We're good enough to afford all of this."

His surroundings could not have been more different from the shabby old office in which he'd worked as a prosecutor. And yet, somewhere deep down, he missed that.

On Thursday afternoon, Nicholas met with Ross Webster in the conference room to go over a Colby, Inc., case currently in litigation. They were seated at a carved walnut table so heavy Nicholas could not imagine how it had ever been moved in one piece.

Ella Fralin had filed suit claiming that the custom-built house she'd purchased from Colby, Inc., had been built with materials substandard to those depicted in her original contract.

Ross had a different take. "Every piece of material used in that house meets code," he said, leaning back in his chair, his hands a teepee beneath his chin. "It's all legal."

Nicholas frowned. "But she says the original proposal laid out a different scenario."

"The misunderstanding lies in the fact that her scenario would have cost a great deal more than what she paid for the house." Ross made the explanation as if Nicholas were a first-year law student in need of a play-by-play.

Nicholas peeled back a couple of pages in the file before him, scanning one of the letters. "Mrs. Fralin alleges the price she paid was to have included the higher-grade materials."

"She's nearly eighty years old," Ross said, starting to sound a little tired of the conversation. "We have the documentation to back up our argument. It'll be an easy sell for a jury to see how she might have misunderstood."

A knock sounded in the open doorway. Sylvia

Webster stepped into the room on a cloud of expensive perfume. She waved a bag at Ross. "New tie delivery."

Ross looked at Nicholas and flipped up the tie he was wearing. "Coffee spill."

Sylvia glanced over her shoulder. "Look who I brought with me."

Behind her, Audrey Colby appeared in the doorway.

Nicholas's stomach took a high dive and hit concrete.

Her hands clasped the strap of her purse as if it were an anchor, the only thing keeping her from running. "Hello," she said, her gaze not quite meeting either his or Ross's.

"Audrey," Ross said, clearing his throat. "How are you?"

"Fine, thanks," she said, her voice measured.

"You've met Nicholas, haven't you?"

She finally looked at him then, her eyes cool, polite. "Yes, briefly."

"It's nice to see you again," Nicholas said.

"You, too." Awkwardness hung in the air, heavy, like imminent snowfall. For the life of him, he couldn't explain why she affected him this way, what it was about her that flattened whatever assurance he'd imagined himself having around women.

"Well," he said, shuffling up the files in front of him and pushing his chair back. "If you'll excuse me, I have some things to finish."

At the doorway, Audrey stepped aside, leaving a notable chunk of distance between them. But even so, he felt the magnetic force field between them as he walked past and wondered if she felt it, too.

CHAPTER SIX

AUDREY AND SYLVIA walked the few blocks from the Webster & Associates office to the Peachtree Plaza Hotel where the Martin Hospice fashion show was to be held at noon. Audrey had considered calling Sylvia and backing out of going today. It had been Jonathan's idea that she should attend. Sylvia was one of the organizers, and the show always received favorable press coverage. Not going, though, would mean an inevitable confrontation.

The detour to Ross's office had been a last-minute surprise. Sylvia had insisted Audrey come in and say hello. Since she couldn't come up with any plausible excuse not to, she'd done so while hoping to avoid Nicholas Wakefield. Seeing him had left her shaken. He unnerved her with the way he looked at her, as if he could see right past any walls she might have put up around herself.

The crosswalk light on Peachtree turned red, the midday traffic heavy.

Sylvia glanced at Audrey, a smile touching her mouth. "Do you want to explain that look?"

Audrey adjusted her sunglasses, her gaze on the other side of the street. "What look?"

"The one between you and that delicious Nicholas Wakefield."

"There wasn't any look," Audrey said, still without letting her eyes meet Sylvia's.

"Oh, from where I was standing, there was." Sylvia raised perfectly arched eyebrows. "Come on, Audrey. We might be married, but we're not dead. And you'd have to be not to notice him. Richard Gere in *An Officer and a Gentleman.* That's who he reminds me of. Those eyes and that smile. They could talk a woman into anything." She laughed. "Or maybe out of anything."

The light changed, and they crossed the street, falling in behind a group of businessmen headed inside the Peachtree Hotel. Despite the winter air, Audrey's face felt flushed.

"I'll take your silence as agreement," Sylvia said, pushing the up button for the elevator. "I can tell you one thing. If he looked at me the way he looked at you a few minutes ago, I'd be walking six inches off the ground. But then again, Ross isn't the jealous type. I get the feeling Jonathan is."

"He has nothing to be jealous of," she said.

The elevator opened with a ding. Two women

in dark suits stepped out. Audrey and Sylvia got on. The doors closed.

Sylvia reached in her purse, pulled out a Chanel lipstick and compact, applied fresh color to her mouth, then snapped the mirror closed. "That's your opinion. But if your husband had seen that look, I feel certain he would disagree."

NICHOLAS SPENT the better part of the afternoon deposing the eighty-year-old woman who claimed Colby, Inc., had not built her the house they had contracted to build. Ella Fralin was sharp as a whip, not a single answer veering off course from her original assertions.

Once Mrs. Fralin had left the conference room, Nicholas walked down to Ross's office, leaned one shoulder against the doorjamb and said, "She was pretty convincing."

"Doesn't matter," Ross replied. "We've got the documentation. It'll stand up in court."

Nicholas studied the other attorney for a few moments, wondering why he was having trouble accepting Ross's version of the story. He now worked for Webster & Associates. Certainly, that's where his loyalties should lie.

It was the gut-instinct thing again.

Ross pushed the button on his speaker phone. "Linda?"

"Yes, Mr. Webster."

"I have some papers here that Jonathan Colby needs to sign. I just spoke with his secretary. He's left for the day. Could you run them by his house for me?"

"Certainly," the secretary said.

"I'll be driving right by there," Nicholas said, the words out before he realized he was going to say them.

Ross looked up at him. "You sure?"

"It's not a problem," he said, even as he began to think better of it.

"Never mind, Linda." Ross clicked off the phone and held out a manila envelope.

Nicholas reached for it.

"If he's home, tell him I'll give him a ring in the morning to see what he thinks," Ross said.

Nicholas nodded. "Sure."

"Hi, Daddy."

Ross's daughter stood in the doorway, smiling. Nicholas recognized her from the picture on her father's desk. Tall with glossy dark hair, she wore a fitted pink sweater and the kind of worn-in-the-knees blue jeans that cost a couple of hundred dollars or better.

"I'm not interrupting, am I?" she asked.

"No. Come in, honey," Ross said. "Have you met Nicholas Wakefield?"

"No," she said, flashing Nicholas another smile and sticking out her hand. "I would have remembered."

"Nicholas, my daughter, Laura," Ross said.

Nicholas shook her hand, noticing the confidence in her grip. "Nice to meet you," he said.

"You're the new partner then?"

"Yes," he said, gathering up his files.

"Daddy says you were with the prosecutor's office?"

"That's right."

"Awfully different work, isn't it?"

"Opposite end of the social ladder for the most part," he agreed.

She held his gaze a moment too long. "I won't be going back to grad school until the fourteenth. I'm trying to decide which career path to take. Maybe we could have lunch. I'd love to hear about your work as a prosecutor."

"I'm not sure that world's for you, sweetheart," Ross spoke up.

She looked at her father. "I don't mind getting a little dirt under my fingernails, Daddy."

Nicholas stood for a moment, not certain what he was supposed to do with that. "I should be going."

"I'll call about that lunch," she said, as if his agreement were a given.

He offered her a polite nod, and then headed

back to his own office where he finished up a couple of letters and then decided to leave early. It was the first evening since he'd started that he'd left the office before seven.

He didn't let himself admit why he was doing so today until he'd reached his car in the parking garage. He'd thought about Audrey Colby countless times since New Year's Eve and had given himself as many lectures on the foolishness of it. Seeing her this morning had caught him off guard. His imagination had not favorably enhanced his memory of her. It had been accurate in every detail. She was as beautiful as he remembered.

He'd had a hard time concentrating on the Fralin deposition that afternoon. He kept seeing Audrey's face, smelling the soft scent of her hair when he'd walked past her on his way out the door.

She was a married woman. And not only that, but married to the biggest client represented by his new law firm. Still, he could not deny that he was leaving early for one reason. He hoped that Jonathan wouldn't be home yet. And that Audrey would be the one to answer the door.

NICHOLAS STOPPED his car outside the Colby house. *Impressive* would have been understating it. It was one of the bigger houses in a neighborhood of hotel-size homes. But instead of the stately mansion he'd expected, the house had a cool, modern look, wings jutting off in every direction, enormous windows. Very *Architectural Digest.*

Manila envelope in hand, he got out and rang the doorbell, wishing with sudden good sense that he'd let Ross's secretary drop it off.

Until Audrey opened the door.

He didn't say anything for several seconds. His voice had escaped him. Dressed in khaki pants and an oversize wool sweater, she looked up at him with a surprised expression, her eyes taking him immediate prisoner.

"Hello again," he said.

"Mr. Wakefield." Her voice was cool and less than welcoming.

"Ross asked me to drop this off for Jonathan."

She took the proferred envelope from him, not quite meeting his gaze. "Thank you. I'm sure he'll appreciate it."

For a few awkward moments, they stood silent in the winter darkness. "I wondered about your resolution," he finally said. "How's it going?"

"On track so far."

When she didn't ask the same of him, he said, "Yeah, me, too. But then I usually do all right the first week. You know, to the gym every night, chains on the refrigerator."

Again, they fell silent, and he was hit with the

same feeling he'd had the night of the Websters' party. He was aware of the vulnerability hidden behind the wall of reserve surrounding her. Her eyes again were the giveaway. They were wary and evasive, in the way of a person whose trust in the world around them has been permanently damaged.

A sudden need for self-preservation made him say, "Well. I'd better get going."

"Good night then." She stepped back to close the door and dropped the envelope. The edge hadn't been sealed, and the papers inside slid onto the brick entrance. She bent over to pick them up. He dropped down to help her. The neckline of her sweater fell to the side of her shoulder, revealing a glimpse of smooth white skin marred by a horrible blue bruise.

His hands fell still on the papers, and he stared at her shoulder, unable to take his eyes away.

She noticed and pulled the sweater back in place. "I—a bike accident. I landed on my shoulder."

He studied her for several seconds, before saying, "That must have hurt."

"I'm fine," she said, standing up and shuffling the papers back inside the envelope. She glanced at him for a moment, then looked away. She stepped back inside the house and closed the door, the click sounding final somehow.

Nicholas stood there, his feet refusing to move.

No reason on earth why he shouldn't believe her, but he knew she was lying.

Why? That was the question.

AUDREY WAITED until she heard the car start before letting herself look out the living-room window. The black Porsche 911 eased out of the driveway.

She watched until the taillights disappeared from sight, one hand clutching the envelope, the other resting on her still tender shoulder. She thought of the day all those years ago when Martha Colby had explained away a too-similar bruise, and a queasy feeling of shame washed over her for the lie. But she had seen the question in his eyes. A moment of doubt for which there was no logical explanation. People had accidents all the time.

And yet, he didn't believe her.

She thought of the excuses she'd used over the past few years—oral surgery, a fall from a horse, anything to explain the bruises when she couldn't hide in the house until they'd faded. Most of the time, she simply kept herself away from the world for as long as she could, not wanting anyone to see her swollen eye or the black-and-blue marks on her neck.

In the days since the New Year's Eve party, she'd thought of Nicholas Wakefield several times.

He'd been kind to her that night. She supposed she'd been drawn to that, some starved part of her needing it, yearning for it. Pathetic as that was.

After Sylvia's accusation that morning, Audrey had not let herself go anywhere near thoughts of the man. She was afraid that somehow her awareness of him would show in her face, that Jonathan would sense it.

Crazy as it sounded, Jonathan's rages had never needed truth to ignite them. The mere suggestion of possibility was all he needed.

She had never expected to open the door to find Nicholas Wakefield staring down at her in his well-cut gray suit, a wilted white shirt, tie loosened at his throat.

This time, she let herself remember his voice, its low, even tones, his words, interested and inquiring.

And his looks.

Dark hair, curling slightly at the sides and just a little longer at the back than Ross Webster probably would have preferred. His eyes were a rich brown, a few worry lines at the corners. Even though it had only been a little after six o'clock, he'd needed a shave. She recalled each of these details with detached impartiality. Like someone in a museum appreciating a fine painting or a particularly nice piece of sculpture, she recognized the appeal, but realized that it didn't apply to her own life.

She glanced at the envelope in her hand, a sick feeling settling in her stomach. Jonathan would be home soon. Should she lie and say Ross's secretary dropped it off? No. If he found out the truth, he would accuse her of having something to hide.

And that wasn't a chance she could afford to take.

NICHOLAS HIT the gym that night. He'd renewed his lapsed membership at a club in Buckhead known as a place where people actually came to work out instead of using it as a singles bar. Kyle had agreed to meet him here under the weight of his annual resolution to get back in shape.

He walked through the door a little past eight, gym bag slung over a ham-size shoulder.

Nicholas met him at the check-in counter. "I never thought I'd hear myself say I missed you."

"Of course you did." Kyle slapped him on the back. "I see you haven't gotten any better-looking."

"You, either," he said, grinning.

House music blasted through ceiling-mounted speakers, the rhythm contagious enough to entice even the most dedicated couch potato onto a piece of equipment. Nicholas and Kyle went upstairs and started out on the treadmill.

"What's it like living in the civilized world?" Kyle asked, upping his speed to a slow jog.

"Very civilized."

Kyle smiled. "Not bored already, are you?"

"Nope," Nicholas said, shooting for a convincing note.

"Met any hot women in that fancy law office?"

Nicholas cranked the speed, picking up his pace, his shoes pounding the machine. "Not exactly."

"There's a straight answer."

He kicked the speed higher until he was running six minute miles and dripping sweat.

Kyle gave him a sideways look. "You have cheesecake for lunch, or you got something on your mind?"

"Overactive imagination, I think."

"This about a case?"

"No."

"A woman, then."

Nicholas didn't answer.

"Ah. So who is she?"

He hesitated, and then admitted, "The wife of a client."

Kyle reached for the towel hanging on the side of the treadmill and wiped his dripping face. "So you're looking to stay with W&A long-term?"

"I'm not involved with her."

"But you're thinking about it."

"I'd have to be a monk not to think about it. There's something about her that keeps nagging at me. Like things aren't what they appear. She's got this look in her eyes. You know the one. Things are as bad as they can get, and they're never going to get any better."

Kyle wiped away another onslaught of sweat. "Man, you've got victim's radar. Things in need just automatically veer in your path."

Nicholas decided not to tell him about the dog. "Your point is?"

"You can find bad stuff anywhere you look. So don't look. If I let myself peel back too much of what I see every day, I'd be walking away from it, too."

Nicholas slowed his speed a few notches to start cooling down, his breathing harsh enough to make his chest hurt. Kyle was right. He should do exactly that. But he kept seeing that bruise on her shoulder. Maybe that *could* be explained by a bike-riding accident. That look in her eyes could not.

It was after midnight.

Audrey stood in front of her bathroom mirror, staring at her reflection. She felt disconnected from it, as if the woman looking back at her was someone she did not know. Did not recognize.

Her lower lip was still bleeding, an inch-long gash down the inside. A tear leaked from the corner of her left eye.

At least, thank God, Sammy hadn't been here. He was spending the night with a friend from school.

Audrey touched a finger to her lip. It would probably go down by morning, but the bruises on her arms would linger and deepen.

She dropped to her knees, opened the third drawer of the bathroom vanity, reached inside and pulled loose the cell phone she had taped to the bottom of the second drawer.

She dialed the number, then sat back on the cool tile floor, legs crossed, elbow on one thigh, a hand pushing the hair back from her face.

Her mother answered, groggy with sleep.

"Mama?"

"Audrey? Honey, what is it?"

Sarah Williams was instantly awake; Audrey could hear the alarm now in her voice. "Everything is fine. I just…wanted to talk. I'm sorry to wake you."

There was a rustling sound, as if her mother were sitting up in bed. "You know how glad I am to hear from you. No matter what time it is."

Audrey sat silent, a sudden knot in her throat. With a few words of acceptance, her mother's voice reduced her to childlike vulnerability.

"Are you all right?" her mother asked, the question layered with meaning.

Her parents knew her marriage wasn't perfect.

That she and Jonathan had problems. She'd never told them everything. She yearned to. But she had chosen this life. Without their absolute blessing. To drag them into it, possibly to have something horrible happen because of her…she couldn't.

And so they simply thought she was too wrapped up in her exciting Atlanta life to have time for them. She could count the number of times they had seen Sammy.

"I'm fine," she said. "Just missing you."

"We miss you, too." This time, there was a catch in her mother's voice, and Audrey's heart felt as if it would split in half at the thought that her parents believed she'd rejected them. "How's Sammy?"

"Good," she said. "Growing."

"He must look like a different child since we saw him."

"Yes."

Another stretch of awkward silence. Audrey asked about her father, her brothers and their wives. They were all well. Her father's arthritis acting up now and then. But other than that, no one complained.

"Mama?"

"What is it, Audrey?"

"I just want to tell you how sorry I am. For the way things have turned out."

Now it was her mother who was silent. "Why

does it have to be this way, sweetheart?" she finally asked. "We love you and want to have you back in our lives. Would that be so terrible?"

Audrey squeezed her eyes shut. "No," she said. "It wouldn't."

"I don't understand," she said softly.

"I know." She paused. "Could you do something for me?"

"Of course."

"Do you have an e-mail address?"

"Your father does at work."

"Could you set one up at home?"

"Yes. But Audrey, what's going on?"

"Use this address."

"Let me get a pen." Audrey could hear the nightstand drawer open, and then her mother said, "Okay."

"CL25490. I checked, and it's available." She gave her mother the name of the Internet provider to contact.

"Audrey, you're scaring me. Is something wrong?"

"Please, don't worry. I hope someday I can explain. But not now. Can you just accept that?"

"Do we have a choice?" Sarah asked, sounding incredibly sad.

"I have to go. I'll be in touch soon, okay?"

"Audrey?"

"Hmm?"

"I do love you. That will never change."

"I love you, too." Audrey cut the connection then, not trusting herself to say anything else. She sat there staring at the phone, the pain she had caused her family nearly more than she could bear.

She placed the cell phone back under the cabinet, then sat there on the bathroom floor, elbows on her knees. How could she tell her mother that she should have listened? That her parents had been right?

That the choices she had made twelve years ago had been hers and hers alone.

THE WINE had long since lost its chill, the bucket in which the bottle had been ensconced in ice now held mildly cool water.

Laura stood at the sixth-floor window of Atlanta's downtown Ritz Carlton. Drivers wove their cars from lane to lane on Peachtree Street like amateur Richard Pettys. Beneath the street lights, a man in a tattered coat trailed a well-dressed woman who kept glancing over her shoulder before hurrying inside the revolving door of an office building.

Laura moved away from the window, glancing at the king-size bed. It had been turned down hours ago, chocolates laid out on the pillow, a single rose next to them.

She picked up her cell phone. Punched three for voice mail.

"You have no new messages."

She tossed the phone in her purse.

This game was getting old. If Jonathan thought he could treat her like some slot machine available for play whenever the mood hit him, she would have to show him differently.

She thought of Audrey Colby, no doubt tucked into bed in her Buckhead mansion, and a noose of fury tightened its loop around her heart.

Audrey had what Laura wanted.

Obviously, this was not the way to get it. She'd meant what she'd said to her father on New Year's Eve. She was not willing to settle for second best.

Time to play the next hand.

DESPITE THE DENIALS he'd made to Kyle, Audrey's name was at the center of Nicholas's thoughts throughout the next day, along with a dozen questions that hurled themselves relentlessly at him. His prosecutor's need to look beneath the surface wouldn't let him ignore the details. The way she'd barely look him in the eye, the nervous glances she kept sending over his shoulder, as though expecting her worst nightmare to materialize.

At six o'clock that evening, the phone on his desk buzzed. "Nicholas Wakefield."

"Nicholas. Hi. It's Laura Webster."

"Laura," he said, surprised.

"Tell me you're bored to tears and wishing for something to do tonight?"

Nicholas pressed two fingers to the headache pulsing in his left temple. Her voice held a subtext of subtle flirtatiousness. "I guess that depends on why you're asking."

"I was hoping you'd take pity on a dateless girl and be my escort to a United Way fund-raiser tonight."

"I'm sure you have a black book an inch thick."

"Compliment, right?"

"Truth more likely."

Laura laughed a not-displeased laugh. "Okay. I feel like this is definite progress."

"Laura. I'm not sure it's a good idea—"

"No strings. You'd just be doing a girl a favor. You might even surprise yourself and have fun," she said.

At another time, he'd have argued his case for Better Not. But the thought of spending another night seeking physical exhaustion as a means of outpacing this sudden gnawing for an explanation to the contradictions he'd observed in Audrey Colby held less than little appeal.

And so he changed his mind. "What time should I pick you up?"

AUDREY HAD DRESSED for the United Way Board of Directors' dinner with the kind of deliberation that signified the event was one to be endured. All social events had become this for her, minefields to be negotiated carefully, a misstep resulting in unthinkable consequence.

Jonathan had chosen to drive tonight, his mood heavy enough that he hadn't bothered to criticize her choice in dress, to suggest to her that it was too low, too clingy, too something.

From their home, it was only a short distance to the Ritz Carlton in Buckhead. Jonathan asked how her day was, and the question sounded so normal that Audrey fought an overwhelming urge to laugh at the ridiculousness of it. It occurred to her then, as it had many times before, that it was normal to Jonathan.

This was the thought most horrifying to her. That Sammy could grow up to believe there was nothing wrong with what he witnessed in his home.

Audrey tightened the lapels of her coat and stared out the window at the expensive houses rolling by, turning her thoughts away from things she could not control.

Jonathan stopped the car in front of the hotel.

Two valets trotted over and opened their doors with welcoming smiles. "Good evening, Mr. Colby. Welcome back to the Ritz."

"Thank you, Marshall," Jonathan said, handing the man a tip. "Park her well, will you?"

From the curb, Audrey watched the exchange, struck again by how likeable her husband sounded, at the look of genuine admiration on the valet's face. This was hardly the first time she'd made the observation, but it never failed to surprise her, make her wonder how it could be that only she saw the other side of him.

They had reached the double wooden doors of the hotel's entrance when another car rolled up to the curb, the engine's low rumble striking a chord of recognition. Audrey glanced over her shoulder. Nicholas Wakefield. With Laura Webster in the passenger seat, smiling at him.

Audrey glanced at Jonathan. He had a grim look on his face.

"Shouldn't we go in?" she said, looking at her watch. "We're nearly late."

"It would be rude not to wait and say hello," he said, taking her hand and tucking it inside his arm.

Audrey stood there, wishing she could be any-where else in the world, knowing that he was about to provide Nicholas with a personal show-ing of Jonathan Colby: devoted, loving husband.

Nicholas looked up, and spotting them, raised a hand in greeting.

Laura saw them in the same moment. "Jonathan. Audrey," she said, crossing the pavement and then waiting for Nicholas to join her. "You know Nicholas, of course."

"Yes, we've already spent quite a few billable hours together," Jonathan said, then adding, "My wife, Audrey. Audrey, Nicholas Wakefield, a new partner with…oh, but that's right, you two met when you dropped those files at my house."

Nicholas nodded, his expression cautious, as if he suddenly sensed a trap of some sort. "Nice to see you again."

"We should go in before they start without us," Jonathan said.

Inside the lobby, a small sign indicated the United Way dinner was on the third floor. They all got in to the same elevator, Nicholas and Laura in back, Jonathan and Audrey in front. Audrey kept her back straight, counting the seconds until the doors opened, and they could get out. The space felt airless, and she could feel the attorney's gaze on her, even though she never let herself meet his eyes.

For the remainder of the night, Audrey made sure she was never in a position to be alone with him. Throughout the cocktails preceding dinner, she stayed on the opposite side of the room and breathed a sigh of relief when they finally sat down for dinner several tables apart. She felt his questions, his curiosity. And she prayed that Jonathan would not notice.

SHE WAS AVOIDING him. Why, Nicholas could not have said, but he knew it was true.

He couldn't stop looking at her. Dear God, she was beautiful. But it was more than that, something inexplicable, as if she were a puzzle he kept going back to even though some of the pieces were missing. As a prosecutor, he'd kept a Rubik's cube in his office. When a case had become too consuming or the questions too overwhelming, he'd grab it out of his drawer, working it back and forth until all the colors lined up. That cube had reassured him, reminded him that there was a pattern to things. Logic could be found if you searched long enough.

"She's lovely, isn't she?"

Nicholas glanced at Laura, not bothering to deny that he had been staring. "I'm just curious. There's something about the two of them that doesn't fit."

"The consensus of the female population in greater Atlanta is that she's lucky to have him. He was quite a catch. He had women chasing him for years before he settled down."

"So what was her secret?"

"I've never understood it." Laura's gaze settled

on the front table where Jonathan and Audrey were seated. Her eyes narrowed for a moment, something that looked surprisingly like jealousy flitting across her face.

Jonathan turned just then and looked directly at Laura.

She put a hand on Nicholas's arm. And it felt to him that she very much hoped the other man had noticed.

While they ate their nouvelle cuisine dinner of fifty-cent-piece-size cuts of filet mignon adorned with three runt-of-the-crop potatoes, Laura asked about his work as a prosecutor, hobbies, college. To his own credit, Nicholas did not let his gaze stray to Audrey Colby again. It spooked him a little, this current he felt between them.

Maybe his imagination simply needed an outlet. He had, after all, gone from a career where the daily supply of nothing-is-as-it-appears stories was endless. Maybe the dryness of corporate law had him thirsty for the familiar. *Then pick another subject, Wakefield. Whatever it is you think you might have imagined about Audrey Colby is exactly that. Imagined.*

He had thoroughly convinced himself of this, until the dinner ended, and he went to get Laura's coat from the coat-check room. Jonathan and Audrey stood at the door, waiting for the attendant to return. He had his hand wrapped around her arm just above the elbow. Something about the way he held her didn't look right to Nicholas. It was more of a grip than a touch.

Jonathan glanced up and saw him. He let go of his wife's arm. But it was impossible to miss the white imprint where his fingers had been, standing in stark relief against her pale skin.

CHAPTER SEVEN

AT JUST AFTER ten o'clock, Nicholas drove Laura back to the Buckhead Diner where she had left her car. She suggested going in for a drink, but he pleaded an early morning, so they called it a night.

He'd sensed her disappointment, but he had wanted to be alone, as if by putting miles between himself and what he'd seen at that coat-check room, he could believe there had been nothing to it.

But after Laura pulled away, he sat in his car thinking about what he had seen.

He loosened his collar and dropped his head against the back of the seat.

Not his business. Leave it alone. Clearly, that was the right choice.

Wasn't that exactly why he'd left his job as a prosecutor? Hung up his white hat? He'd given up trying to make the world work in a different way.

What he had seen might not have been what it appeared to be, anyway. Or so he could hope.

AS SOON AS they'd arrived home from the dinner, Jonathan had closed himself in his office. He had been silent throughout the drive, and Audrey said a silent prayer of thanks for the reprieve. She could only assume seeing Laura with Nicholas had bothered him enough to shift the focus away from any transgressions Audrey might have made during the evening.

She stood at the window of Sammy's bedroom, looking out at the backyard, comforted by her son's even breathing. Just the sound of it steadied her, smoothed the edges of the worry making her nearly nauseous. If only she could turn the clock forward to Jonathan's trip, make the days go by. A single opportunity. She wanted it so desperately that the thought of it slipping through her fingers left a metallic taste in her mouth, the taste of potential failure, of hopelessness.

Nicholas Wakefield was a threat to that opportunity. She had seen it in his eyes tonight when she glanced up to find him staring at Jonathan's grip on her arm. Jonathan had been angry, accusing her of flirting with Trent Wilson, the man seated beside her. Audrey knew Trent was very much in love with his wife, but Jonathan was blind to that. She had, after all, smiled at one of the man's jokes.

The impossibility of her position made her feel as if she had concrete attached to her feet, pulling her down with no hope of ever getting her head above water again. For so long, she had prayed that someone would notice, throw her a rope, pull her in. But to the rest of the world, she was floating along, living an idyllic life: pampered, treasured, the wife of a man half the women in Atlanta would have stood in line for had they thought he was available.

Something told Audrey, however, this was not what Nicholas Wakefield saw. She could not explain how she knew, but she felt it. Felt the questions, the concern. And how odd that was, that a virtual stranger felt concern for her.

But she did not want his interference; she hoped that he would forget what he had seen tonight.

For the next few days, she had to hold her existence together, keep the pieces in place. If one, even one, slipped, it might ruin everything. She knew without doubt that this was her last chance. Her only chance. If she failed this time…she could not bear even to think of it.

THAT NIGHT, Nicholas dreamed about Sherry.

Vivid, Technicolor dreams in which her beautiful young face was full of life. He'd taught her how to ride a bike, and that was the day his memory played for him. They'd been in the backyard at the farm, Nicholas, nine, Sherry, seven. She'd taken the lesson as seriously as she had her first day at kindergarten. More than anything, she wanted to ride her bike behind Nicholas down the lane in front of their house. She'd caught on amazingly fast, from sheer will their mother said later. Her mission in life, from the time she could walk, was to keep up with Nicholas. When she had mastered the backyard, they'd gone out to the front of the house, their bikes side by side for the first ride down the gravel drive.

"Don't forget about your brakes," Nicholas said. "If you need to slow down, just tap on them."

Sherry frowned, some of her confidence wavering. "What if they don't work?"

It was a question Nicholas had never considered. He puzzled over it a moment, and then said, "Just put your feet on the handlebars, and let her roll."

Nicholas woke abruptly, his sister's little-girl giggle echoing in his head.

He raised up on his elbows at a sound from the doorway. The dog stood just across the threshold, watching him. By choice, she slept in the kitchen, refusing the pillow he'd placed a few feet away from his own bed. He still hadn't named her; he couldn't seem to settle on anything that fit. "Guess I woke you, huh?"

She stared at him, unblinking, then lay down outside the door.

Nicholas got out of bed, went into the bathroom and took a couple of Excedrin to kill the headache beating at his temples. The man staring back at him in the mirror looked as if he hadn't bothered to go to bed at all.

Over the years, he could count the number of times he'd dreamed about Sherry, her presence denied to him even in his sleep. The few times he had dreamed of her were when he was especially bothered about a case, when the injustice of a wrong would not leave him alone.

He had fallen asleep a few hours ago with Audrey Colby's face firmly imprinted in his mind, the stain of her husband's fingerprints on her arm an image that looped through his thoughts on permanent repeat.

He could deny it all he wanted, tell himself things weren't always what they seemed. But he'd listened to his gut too long to ignore it this time. And he knew what his gut was telling him.

The injustice of a wrong.

Nicholas saw his sister's face again, suspended in youth. He hadn't let himself think of that night for a long time. He'd blocked it from his thoughts because that was the only way he'd been able to find his way forward. But there was something about Audrey Colby that prodded him to look back, as if there were something he had forgotten and needed to remember.

THE LAST THING Nicholas had wanted to do was pick his little sister up after the football game that Friday night. He had a date with Maria Reed. They'd been seeing one another for about two months, and he had a feeling that night would be *the* night. He'd looked forward to their date all week, sitting in his senior calculus class day-dreaming about her creamy skin and long legs.

No week had ever passed so slowly. And on Friday morning, when his mother had asked him to give Sherry a ride after the game, he'd done his best to get out of it.

"Mom, I've got plans," he'd argued from the breakfast table where he'd been racing his way through a bowl of cereal.

"Son, your father and I won't be out of the symphony until after eleven. The game will be over by ten at the latest. And since your sister is still grounded for being late last week, I'm sticking to my guns on her not riding home with friends."

Nicholas shot a glance at Sherry who was glaring at their mother, her dark hair falling over one shoulder, her blue eyes full of fire. At fifteen, she was beautiful and headstrong in a way that redefined the words *willful teenager.* "Oh, Mom, can't I just ride home with Beth and Suzie?"

"This is not open for discussion, young lady. If you weren't cheering at the game, you'd be staying at home tonight," Charlotte Wakefield said. Their mother was not the strictest of disciplinarians. Even though her limits could be tested a lot farther than most of the moms Nicholas knew, Sherry had stepped over the line this time. Her curfew was midnight, and when she'd straggled in at two-thirty the previous Saturday night, his mother had been pacing the floor, certain she was lying in a ditch somewhere, bleeding to death.

Sherry's excuse had been weak. And even though Nicholas was only a little over two years older than his sister, he'd already learned how frantic his parents could get if he didn't show up on time or at least call. Sherry hadn't yet learned that.

"Mom, I've got a date," he tried again. "With Maria. I haven't seen her all week—"

"You'll still see her. You just have to pick up your sister after the game," she said, her tone final.

He slid back his chair, leaving his cereal unfinished. "Next time you get grounded, pick a better weekend, Sher."

"Oh, you're just mad because you think you might not get to make out with Maria," Sherry said.

"Sherry," her mother warned. "You're the one being punished here. Not your brother."

"You could have fooled me," Nicholas mumbled.

Sherry shot out of her chair and stomped off down the hall to get her books.

"Nicholas, I'm sorry to mess up your plans, but if I don't stand by this, she'll never learn that there's a price to pay for her actions."

Some not-yet-ready-to-admit-it part of himself knew his mother was right.

"You'll do this for me, won't you?" she asked.

"Yeah, Mom, I'll do it," he said, before heading out the door.

MARIA'S PARENTS were out of town for the weekend. She'd invited Nicholas over for dinner, a meal she'd cooked herself after asking him what his favorite things were. When he arrived at her house just after six, he could smell the aroma of roast beef wafting in from the kitchen.

But as he stared at Maria dressed in a pair of close-fitting blue jeans and a black blouse with a rounded neckline that hinted at cleavage, the last thing on his mind was food.

"Hi," she said, smiling.

"You look great," he said, smiling back, putting his hands on her narrow waist and pulling her close. He leaned against the door, and they kissed for a long time, both of them forgetting about everything except the fact that they'd been driving one another crazy the past two months by doing everything but going all the way. The kissing got wilder, and he ran his hands along her back, before coming around to cup her breasts, the ache inside him growing heavier by the moment. The buzzer sounded. They ignored it for several seconds, until Maria said, "I better get that. Don't want the house to catch on fire."

"Yeah," he said, following her into the kitchen and helping get the roast beef out of the oven. Maria had swiped a bottle of wine from her parents' supply. Nicholas managed to get the bottle open and poured them both a glass. They sipped at it, laughing about some of the things that had happened at school that week, and actually got as far as mashing the potatoes before they started kissing again.

She unbuttoned his shirt and slid her hands inside, driving him crazy with her touch. He didn't think he could stand it if they stopped this time, and to his great relief, Maria took his hand and led him from the kitchen, saying, "We can eat later. I don't think this can wait."

He followed her up the stairs to her room where she closed the door behind them and locked it. Nicholas had made out with a couple of girls, but both encounters had been of the experimental variety. With Maria, he wanted it to be more than that. He wasn't sure he knew what love was, but this felt like every description he'd ever heard. He stood there looking at her for several seconds, appreciating her soft curves and open, inviting expression.

They started kissing again, their breathing harsh and headed toward out of control.

Nicholas picked her up and laid her in the middle of her bed, sweeping aside the stuffed animals at the top. He unsnapped her jeans, his hand splayed on the flat of her belly, while she pushed his shirt from his shoulders.

None of the foreplay they'd been practicing for weeks had prepared Nicholas for the reality of making love. It was better than anything he'd ever imagined.

"How many more times can you do it?" Maria asked with a laugh, lying back against the pillow, the sheet barely covering her breasts.

"How many times can you?" he questioned in return, smiling. He glanced at the clock and then groaned. Nine-thirty. "I've gotta go."

"What is it?" Maria asked, wrapping an arm around his waist, her head on his shoulder.

"I have to pick Sherry up at ten."

"Tonight?" Maria couldn't hide her disappointment.

"She's grounded, and Mom asked me to give her a ride after the game."

"But I thought—"

He rolled over and scooped her up against him, loving the feel of her naked body next to his. "I'm sorry. I tried to get out of it, but Mom wasn't giving on this one."

Maria sighed and said, "Just a few more minutes."

Nicholas glanced at the clock again. Nine-thirty-five. "I really should go."

Her face settled into disappointment. "My parents will be home tomorrow. Who knows when we'll have another chance like this?"

Nicholas groaned. "Yeah," he said. "Who knows?"

MARIA WENT with him to pick up Sherry at the high school. It was almost ten-thirty. He was only a half hour late and already most of the parking lot was empty. He drove down to the gymnasium door where he'd told Sherry he would meet her. He didn't see her right away, so he pulled the Jeep under one of the overhead lights and turned off the ignition.

He looked at his watch and then at Maria who had her hand on his leg. "I wonder where she is."

"Maybe she's inside."

"Yeah. Let me go look. I'll be right back."

Nicholas got out and went inside the gym. No one was in sight, but he called out, "Sherry?"

"Can I help you?" The school janitor, an older man with stooped shoulders, appeared from behind the bleachers, a broom in his hand.

"I'm looking for my sister. Sherry Wakefield. She was supposed to meet me outside the gym a little while ago."

"Haven't seen anyone in the last twenty minutes or so. What's she look like?"

"Dark hair. Blue eyes. Probably wearing a leather aviator jacket."

"Oh, yeah. Pretty little girl. She was here maybe thirty, forty minutes ago. Said she was waiting for her brother. I told her she could wait inside, but she said she'd be fine and went on out."

Nicholas frowned. Maybe she'd gotten tired of waiting and left with some of her friends. "Was anyone else with her?"

The janitor bent to pick up a gum wrapper. "Nope. Most everyone had gone by then."

"Thanks."

"Sure thing," the man said.

Nicholas went back to the Jeep and opened the door. "Any sign of her?" he asked Maria.

She shook her head. "She wasn't inside?"

"No. Where is she?" It would be just like Sherry to take off with some of her friends and forget he was waiting for her. But then Mom had been specific about her not doing that, and he didn't think even Sherry would have pushed this one. He glanced around the dark parking lot again and then got inside the Jeep. "I guess we should wait a little while and see if she comes back."

"Okay," Maria said, then leaned over and kissed him. "Hey, don't be so hard on her. She'll probably be right back. And we were late."

Nicholas knew she was right, but he was getting a little uneasy. It was almost eleven. An hour since they were supposed to meet. They waited until eleven-fifteen. By then, Nicholas was really worried. Sherry knew their folks would be home anytime, and he knew she wouldn't want to come in after they did.

"Let's drive through town," he said, running a hand through his hair. They left the high school and headed for the mall where some of the kids hung out in the parking lot on weekends. Nicholas stopped the Jeep by a group of cars he recognized and lowered the window. A friend of Sherry's came forward, recognizing him.

"Hey, Tina. Have you seen Sherry?"

"After the game, she was waiting outside the gym. We asked her if she wanted a ride. She said she was grounded, and you were picking her up."

A knot began to form in Nicholas's stomach. "Yeah. I was running late."

Tina glanced at Maria and waved, a knowing smile on her face. "She wasn't there when you went by?"

Nicholas shook his head. "I'll go and check again. Maybe she's there by now."

"Okay. See you later."

Nicholas waved, and they drove back to the high school. There were no cars in the lot now, and it was eerily quiet as he got out and called her name even though no one was in sight.

He went to the pay phone outside the gymnasium door, dialed his home number with a feeling of dread. He glanced at his watch. Eleven forty-five. By now, he didn't even care about the trouble he was going to be in for being late. He just wanted to hear that Sherry was home.

His mother answered the phone.

"Mom?"

"Hi, honey, I thought you two would be back by now. We just got in the door."

The dread inside Nicholas spread, and a few seconds passed before he could bring himself to say the words. "I can't find her, Mom. I was late picking her up, and she wasn't there."

"What do you mean she wasn't there, Nicholas?"

"I thought she might have left with some of her friends, so I drove around, but no one has seen her since they left the game."

"Where are you, son?"

"At the gym. In the parking lot."

"Stay right there," she said, her voice somber. "Your father and I will be there in a few minutes."

They waited in silence until his parents' car pulled into the spot beside the Jeep. Nicholas's father got out, his expression troubled. "No sign of her?"

Nicholas shook his head. "I didn't know what to do, Dad. I was late getting here." He shot a guilty glance at Maria who looked down at the pavement. "I'm sorry, Dad." He explained then what the janitor had said as well as Sherry's friend Tina.

Taylor Wakefield put a hand on Nicholas's shoulder and said, "There's got to be an explanation. You and Maria take the south end of town. See if anyone's seen her. Your mom and I will take the north end. Let's meet back here in twenty minutes."

Nicholas glanced at his parents' car where his mother sat in the front seat, looking more worried than he'd ever seen her. They all knew this wasn't like Sherry.

He and Maria did as his father suggested, but again to no avail. No one had seen her.

Twenty minutes later, when they all met back at the same spot, his parents' faces were grave with concern. They both got out of the car, his father saying, "We've called home twice to make sure she wasn't there. No answer. I'm going to call the police. I know they'll say she hasn't been missing long enough, but I don't know what else to do."

Missing. The word hit Nicholas with the force of a tractor trailer. This couldn't be happening. He'd been late. But what could have happened in thirty minutes?

Charlotte Wakefield came over and put her arm around him. "Everything's going to be all right."

Nicholas loved his mother more in that moment than he'd imagined loving her. He knew how scared she was, how upset she must be with him. But she'd sensed his guilt and fear, and rather than blame him, she consoled him.

Taylor went to the pay phone and called the sheriff's department. Within five minutes, a patrol car pulled into the parking lot beside them, Sheriff Wally Akers getting out and nodding to them. "Taylor. Charlotte. What's the problem?"

"It's Sherry. Nicholas was supposed to pick her up at ten. He was late getting here, but no one has seen her since a little before then."

"You sure she didn't decide to leave with friends?"

"We've both driven around and asked the kids in town. She wasn't with any of them."

Nicholas supposed that in some places, the police would have said there was nothing they could do yet. But in a town like the one in which they lived, there was nothing normal about a missing fifteen-year-old girl. Wally went back to the car, reached for his radio and said something into the speaker.

Maria moved closer to Nicholas and took his hand, squeezing it with the same fear he himself was feeling.

Two more squad cars arrived with their lights flashing. The police asked his parents a lot of questions about Sherry's habits, what kind of child she was, whether there was a possibility she could have run away.

Nicholas watched his mother's face grow more and more ashen, and when the police asked what Sherry had been wearing, she could barely get the words past her lips. Once they'd finished with the questions, Wally suggested that they go home and wait in case Sherry showed up there. "There's nothing you can do here. We've put out an APB for her, and the minute we hear something, we'll call you."

They left, reluctantly. Nicholas drove Maria home, and as they pulled up in front of her house, she turned to him with tears trailing down her face. "I'm sorry, Nicholas. I feel like this is my fault. If I hadn't asked you to stay longer—"

"It's not your fault, Maria," he said, his voice heavy.

She leaned across the seat and kissed him. "I'll say a prayer for her. Please call me as soon as you hear something."

"I will," Nicholas promised.

He drove home then, still not quite able to believe this was happening. He went inside the house where his parents were waiting in the den by the phone.

He sat down on the couch, his hands on his knees, his gaze on the floor. "I'm sorry, Mom and Dad. If anything's happened to her, I don't know how—"

"Nicholas. Don't say such things," his mother said quietly, crossing the room to put her arm around his shoulders. "Let's pray for the best and not think about anything else."

Nicholas looked up at his father who nodded and said, "She's right, son. This is no time for blame."

They waited throughout the night, drinking coffee and willing the phone to ring, yet dreading it more with each hour that passed. It was just after 6:00 a.m. when a knock sounded at the front door. Taylor Wakefield jumped up and went to answer it. Charlotte and Nicholas followed close behind.

Sheriff Akers stood there in the early morning light, his hat in his hand. Harry Clark, one of the local doctors, at his side.

"Taylor, I'm afraid I've got some bad news for you."

Charlotte put a hand to her mouth, a moan escaping her lips. "Oh, no. No."

Nicholas caught her as she began to faint. Taylor stepped back and put his arm around her, holding her up. Nicholas moved away, trying to swallow and yet unable to for the fear lodged in his throat.

"Tell us, Sheriff. Where is she?" Taylor demanded.

"She's dead, Taylor," Sheriff Akers said in a stricken voice. "Dear Lord, I'm sorry, but she's dead."

Charlotte slumped to the floor. Taylor leaned over and picked her up in his arms, tears streaming down his face.

Dr. Clark stepped inside and said, "Let's get her upstairs, Taylor. I've got something I can give her."

Nicholas stood frozen in the same spot, unable to think, not feeling anything except the awful realization that this wasn't a dream, that he wasn't going to wake up, that he couldn't go back and redo last night. A half hour. That was all. Dear God, please don't let this be true. Please give me another chance. I won't be late this time. I'll give up however many years you want me to if you'll just give me back that half hour so Sherry will be safe. Please, God. Just a half hour.

Nicholas didn't know how much time had

passed before he heard his father's voice from the top of the stairs. "No, Wally. I have to see her."

"I don't think it's a good idea, Taylor."

"I have to see her." His father was halfway down the stairs then. He looked at Nicholas and said, "I'm going with Wally, son. You stay here with your mother, all right?"

Of all times, Nicholas knew he should have listened to his father. But he couldn't. He had to see her for himself, or he didn't think he'd ever believe it could be real. Maybe they were wrong. Maybe it wasn't Sherry. "I want to go with you, Dad. Please."

Taylor hesitated for several seconds, his grief-stricken face making it clear that he didn't have the strength to deny his son.

They rode in Wally's squad car to the track where they'd found Sherry's body. In a low voice, Wally told them an early-morning runner had spotted her just an hour ago. Nicholas heard the words as if they had been issued through some muffling device. The track. But that couldn't be. It was only a few hundred yards from the gymnasium. Up on the hill. Why hadn't Sherry heard him when he'd called her?

An ambulance and three other police cars were waiting for them. Wally pulled up beside them. Taylor looked at Nicholas in the back seat and said, "Stay here, son. We'll be right back."

Nicholas nodded, hearing and seeing what was taking place around him, but feeling completely separated from it. He watched his father walk toward the scene, stop and stare down at what he saw there, before listing forward like a ship that is about to sink beneath the waves.

Nicholas got out of the car and ran to the spot where two men gripped his father's arms.

Lying behind one of the mats the track team used for practice was his fifteen-year-old sister. Her beautiful face was bruised and swollen, and if she hadn't been wearing his old aviator jacket, he wouldn't have believed it was her. The short cheerleading skirt she'd been wearing was up around her waist. Her thighs were bruised and bloody.

Nicholas felt as if he couldn't breathe, as if he were in the middle of a nightmare so terrible that it couldn't possibly be true.

But it wasn't a nightmare. It was real.

Sherry was dead.

And it was his fault. His fault.

CHAPTER EIGHT

NICHOLAS STOOD under the shower for a long time, trying to find the energy to move. His body felt heavy with the weight of the memories. It was a place he hadn't let himself go in many, many years.

His sister's killer had never been found.

This was what he'd never been able to accept: that the cruelty of one human being could go unpunished, could continue to be perpetuated against others.

Throughout his career, this was the hole he'd been trying to fill, but never could. It was as though the bottom had its own trap door, and no matter how much good he tried to pile in on top, the trap always gave way, and he was left with the same emptiness, the same feeling of failure.

As a prosecutor, he'd taken every case personally. Felt the pain of the victims' family as if it were his own. Because he knew what they were feeling.

And that made it impossible to ignore the little

voice inside him where Audrey Colby was concerned. He'd seen Jonathan's grip on her arm last night, knew with bone-deep certainty that her life was nothing like it appeared to be.

He wanted to ignore it.

And knew with absolute certainty that he could not.

JONATHAN LEFT the house early the next morning, before Audrey came downstairs. After dropping Sammy off at school, she drank two cups of coffee at the Starbucks on Peachtree while she waited for the mall to open. At two minutes before ten, she got in her car and drove across the street to Lenox Square. She started at the department store on the end, buying dresses, shoes and lingerie.

The leggy blond saleslady stacked the items by the cash register. "You must be going somewhere special," she said, slipping a protective bag over one of the dresses.

"Yes," Audrey said. "I am."

A few minutes later, receipt in hand, she took everything out to the car and then headed for the next store on her list.

By twelve o'clock she had filled both the trunk and the back seat with bags. She then went home to unpack.

As THE NEW guy on the block, Nicholas had inherited a batch of cases no one else in the office wanted to mess with. It was all pain-in-the-neck stuff, conjuring the kind of tedium that made him think chewing glass would be a nice alternative.

At just after noon, he walked down the hall to Ross's office with a file in his hand, determined not to let his irritation show. He'd e-mailed the attorney twice the day before and twice again this morning with the same question. He still hadn't received an answer.

Nicholas stuck his head inside the slightly open door. Ross was on the phone, but waved him in and pointed at a chair. Nicholas sat and picked up within seconds that he was talking to Colby.

Once Ross had hung up, Nicholas stood and held up the file. "You get an answer?"

Ross ran a hand over his face. "Sorry. I forgot to ask him about those leases. Why don't you give him a call? He's at the office."

Nicholas nodded and made his way back down the hall. He stood in front of his desk for a moment, weighing the wisdom, or lack thereof, in what he was about to do.

He looked at the number in the file, then buzzed his secretary and told her he was going to lunch.

HE TOOK the interstate out to Buckhead, pulled into the parking lot of a 7-Eleven, picked up his cell phone and dialed Colby's number. The secretary put him through.

"Jonathan, Nicholas here. Got a couple of questions for you."

"I have a meeting here in five minutes," Colby replied in a curt voice.

"Five minutes is all I need."

Nicholas got his answers and made some quick notes in the file. He tossed his cell phone on the passenger seat and wheeled out onto the road.

AUDREY PARKED her car at the front of the house. She would take some of the bags upstairs for Jonathan to see. He loved for her to buy things. He took it as a symbol of her forgiveness.

She glanced at her watch. Less than an hour before she had to pick up Sammy. She grabbed several bags from the back seat, then hurried up the front steps of the house.

A car downshifted and slowed at the end of the driveway. Audrey glanced over her shoulder.

She let go of the bags, and they dropped to the stone entryway at her feet. She could feel her heart pounding. What was he doing here? Meeting Jonathan? Leaving something for him again?

Audrey closed her eyes for a second and forced

herself to take a deep breath. *Don't overreact. Just see what he wants. Tell him you have to leave, and he'll be on his way.*

He pulled in behind her, and it occurred to her that she would never again hear this particular car and not think of him. The thought was so unexpected, so out of place that she stood, transfixed, while he cut the engine and got out.

"Hello," he said, looking unsure of his reception.

"Is there something I can help you with, Mr. Wakefield?" She heard the coolness in her voice, saw it change the expression on his face and knew the word he would probably use to describe her.

"Do you have a minute to talk?"

"No, actually, I don't. I have to pick up my son."

He wore a dark-navy suit and a light-blue shirt, his tie loosened at his throat, as if he tolerated the notion of respectability but never quite gave it his full endorsement. He shoved his hands in the pockets of his pants, the action strangely out of synch with the confident attorney she had seen at the Ritz Carlton the night before. "I won't take up much of your time."

"I'm afraid I don't have any to offer you, Mr. Wakefield."

He moved closer, stopping just short of the steps, his uncertainty a stumbling block to the icy unwelcome she'd intended to project. If Jonathan came home…if one of the neighbors mentioned having seen the car in the drive…

"Don't worry," he said. "He's in a meeting. I made sure before I came."

The words shocked Audrey into silence, their implication kickstarting her heart into overdrive again. "Come inside," she said, turning her key in the lock and pushing open the door. He followed her in and shut it behind him.

She dropped the bags at her feet and whirled on him, so caught off guard that she didn't take the time to censor the fear and anger from her voice. "What are you doing?"

"Audrey—"

"You don't know me. You have no idea what you're doing."

"You're right," he said. "I don't. But if you need help—"

"I don't want your help." Her voice rose with sudden panic. "What I meant is I don't need your help. What would make you think such a thing?"

He stared at her for a few long seconds, glanced at his feet, then met her eyes again. "I know it seems crazy. It *feels* crazy to me, but since we met, I've just had this feeling that…maybe you do."

It was all Audrey could do to stand there and not let the emotions raging through her show on her face. The kindness in his voice nearly buckled her knees. For so long she had prayed that someone would see…

But not now. And not this man.

She pressed her lips together, reaching for composure. "Mr. Wakefield, there is only one thing I want from you. And that is for you to leave. Whatever it is you think you've imagined is exactly that. Imagined. Now please, go."

She opened the door, stood to the side and waited for him to move. He held her gaze for several unnerving moments, his eyes dropping to her shoulder and the now-concealed bruise she had explained away when he had been here before. He stepped outside then, looking at her open car and the bags visible in the back seat and trunk. "So I guess I had it all wrong," he said.

"Yes," she replied. "Obviously, you did."

He walked to his car, opened the door and got inside. She watched him drive away. And for some inexplicable reason, she wanted to go after him, to tell him all those material things meant nothing to her. That tomorrow she would return every single bag to the store from which it had been purchased and ask for cash.

HE'D SEEN it with his own eyes.

So why was he having trouble believing that Audrey Colby was the kind of woman who didn't mind being slapped around in exchange for a life of unlimited shopping?

He pulled into a Texaco and cut the engine at the unleaded tank. He popped the gas latch, then got out and swiped his AmEx through the credit card machine. He stood with his back against the car while the gas ran, arms folded across his chest.

Outside the store, two teenage boys argued over rightful ownership of a lottery ticket they'd gone in on. From the corner of his eye, he saw the BMW whip by, Audrey's blond hair a blur.

His response was automatic. He popped the nozzle out of the tank, hung it up and slapped the cap back on the car. The machine beeped its take-your-receipt reminder, but he left it hanging and jumped in.

He pulled out in front of a truck onto West Paces Ferry road, the driver hitting his horn.

She was nowhere in sight, so Nicholas stepped on the gas, not letting himself consider what he was doing or why.

Half a minute later, he spotted her two cars ahead.

He hit the brake and hung back. At the light she went right onto Filmore.

He was three cars behind now. A catering service van crawled along in front of him, blocking his view. A mile or so later, the van took a left. He waited behind it with increasing impatience.

With the van out of the way, he had a clear view now. But she was nowhere in sight. He drove on another couple of minutes, not spotting her.

He did a U-turn and headed in the other direction down Filmore. He glanced back and forth between the buildings on either side of the road. He was just about to give up when he spotted the BMW in a parking lot. He hit his blinker and pulled into a space a few rows down from her car.

The sign on the building read Buckhead Trace-Matherson Library.

So what? Had he thought she might be driving to the nearest women's shelter, proving that he was right?

Maybe he had been wrong. Maybe her life *was* that normal. Returning overdue books for her son.

And he was following her.

He was starting to scare himself.

He circled the lot, found the exit and drove back to the office.

AUDREY TOOK the elevator to the second floor, walked quickly to the computer section, taking a station on one end. She logged on, accessed her e-mail account and sat for a few moments, heart pounding, until the screen popped up.

You have new mail.

A fine sheen of sweat broke out on her forehead and upper lip. She clicked on the icon.

We have identified a secure location for you and your son. I have attached a schedule with the details of your destination. You should arrive at Atlanta Hartsfield International on February 7th. Go to the Triple Scoop on Concourse A. At 9:00 a.m., order your son a chocolate ice cream. Ask the server to make sure there are no nuts because he's allergic. That will be the server's cue to give you your tickets. Once you've received those, go to the British Airways terminal. Your flight will depart at 12:00 p.m. The envelope will contain train tickets as well as instructions for the remainder of your journey.

Good luck.

Kathryn Millborn

Audrey sat completely still, stunned. So simple. It sounded so simple. Could it possibly be?

A flutter of hope took wing inside her. And for the first time in so long, it felt real.

NICHOLAS DREAMED about Sherry again that night. But this time she wasn't alone. Audrey was with her. He saw the two of them walking together. He tried to call out to them, but they couldn't hear him.

He started to run after them, as fast as he could, his lungs screaming for relief. But he couldn't catch up. They stayed the same distance ahead of him, no matter how fast he ran. He finally stopped, gasping for air and still trying to call out to them. *Stop! Wait!* But his voice had grown weaker, and he knew there was no chance they would hear him now.

Nicholas sat straight up in bed. He was soaked in sweat, his heart racing as if he had actually been running.

As she had the night before, the dog came to the open doorway of the room, her ears perked.

Nicholas swung out of bed and got in the shower, standing under the pounding spray until the dream receded, and his heart rate slowed to normal.

When he came back out to get dressed, the dog lay curled up on the pillow next to his bed. She raised her head once to look at him, her expression accepting, as if she had finally decided to trust him.

When Sherry had been six or seven years old, she'd wanted a dog more than anything in the world. His parents had told her she wasn't yet old enough, so she made up an imaginary one. Set up water bowls in the kitchen and upstairs bathroom. Played in the backyard with a pet no one else could see but her.

Nicholas heard her voice in his head then, clear as yesterday, calling her imaginary dog in for dinner.

"Lola," he said, reaching down to pat the dog stretched out on the pillow beside him. "That name okay with you?"

The dog licked the back of his hand.

"I'll take that as a yes," he said.

NICHOLAS DIDN'T NEED to be told that it would be wise to follow Audrey's wishes and leave her alone.

But he could focus on nothing else. It was as if he'd been injected with a drug so addictive that all he could think about was getting the next fix.

At six o'clock that evening, the office had nearly cleared out. He got up from his desk and closed his door. He dialed Kyle's direct number. Kyle never left work before seven. He answered on the second ring.

"Hey," Nicholas said.

"Let me guess. You want your job back."

"I haven't thrown in the corporate towel just yet."

"Can't deny I'm disappointed. I'm beginning to realize what a load you carried around here."

"Thanks, Kyle."

"This isn't a social call, is it?"

"No. A favor, actually. I need to know if you've got anything in the computer on Jonathan Colby."

HIS PHONE RANG just over an hour later.

"I found a couple of things for you," Kyle said. "Buy me dinner, and I'll tell you about it."

"Ernesto's?"

"Twenty minutes."

"I'll see you there," he said and hung up.

ERNESTO'S WAS a quiet little Italian place in the heart of downtown Atlanta. Not so big on atmosphere, but the food was unbeatable.

Kyle sat at a table by the window. Nicholas took the chair across from him. "Hey, thanks for meeting me."

"Anything for a free meal."

The waiter came and took their orders. As soon as they were alone, Kyle picked up his briefcase and pulled out a file. He handed it over.

Nicholas opened it and scanned the pages inside, then looked up. "Two incidents?"

"Neighbors called in one. An emergency-room doctor the other."

"And why were the charges dropped?"

"Because Mrs. Colby refused to go through with

it." Kyle hesitated, and then said, "The woman you mentioned at the club. She's the one, isn't she?"

Nicholas didn't say anything.

Kyle reached for a roll. "Cape's back out of the closet, huh?"

"It's not like that," he denied.

"Right."

"I don't know," Nicholas said, running a hand over his face. "I can't get her out of my head."

"Man, are you sure you know what you're doing?" Kyle said, his voice laced with genuine concern.

"I didn't go looking for it."

"Didn't say you did."

They were both quiet for a few moments.

"Are you interested in this woman?" Kyle finally asked, sitting back and folding his arms across his chest.

"She's married."

"Glad you noticed." Kyle sighed, took a few sips from his water glass. "You know, you're not the ugliest guy in the world. There are single women out there who would probably say yes to a dinner invitation. Trouble is you don't ask any of them."

Nicholas frowned. "You make it sound like I've never been out on a date."

Kyle raised an eyebrow. "Yeah, you take women out. But dating usually involves a succession of evenings—emphasis on the word *succession*—spent together, the result something sometimes known as commitment. *That* I've never seen you do."

"Maybe I've never met the right woman," he said.

"What?" Kyle said. "You don't like being under my microscope?"

"As a matter of fact, no."

"Okay, Nick, so look, you don't talk about it much, but I know you've had some bad stuff in your life. Losing a sister the way you did…there aren't any words for it."

"Kyle—"

"Hear me out," he said. "I think that was the fire inside you as a prosecutor. And somewhere along the line, you stopped believing you were making a difference. That's where you're wrong. I've never worked with anyone who made more of a difference than you did."

Nicholas looked away, swallowing hard. "Thanks."

"Is that what you're doing with this woman?" Kyle asked in a soft voice.

He met his friend's gaze, started to deny it, then stopped. "I don't know," he said.

"Maybe that's something you ought to figure out before you go any further with this."

"Yeah," he said, wishing he could deny it.

CHAPTER NINE

ON THURSDAY MORNING, Audrey dropped Sammy off at school, then drove downtown to the City Gardener, parking in the lot next to the shop.

She got out of her car and opened the trunk, breathing a sigh of relief. She'd wrapped each of the pots in newspaper and bubble wrap, but a sharp turn could still have caused them to move enough to chip an edge. She pulled the paper back from one of the larger pots and smoothed a finger across the rim.

This last dozen contained some of what she thought were her best pots so far. She'd given up her painting early in her marriage. Jonathan had thought it a waste of time when she could be doing something active like tennis.

One day, she'd decided to spruce up an old flower pot, covering it with a coat of paint and then, on a whim, thinning another color and streaking it over the base. After letting it dry, she had smudged on some burnt umber for antiquing.

When she was done, she sat staring at the pot, loving the muted colors, the layered finish.

It was the first thing in so long that had made her remember the person she had once wanted to be. Jonathan had seen her early efforts, declared them not bad if they never left the storage room of their basement. From that point, she had hidden her work from him, putting a pot out somewhere in the house occasionally just so he wouldn't get suspicious about her hobby as he had defined it.

"Audrey?"

She swung around and found Nicholas Wakefield standing just behind her, holding an oversize briefcase. She touched a hand to her chest, surprised. "What are you doing here?"

"Actually, I'm meeting with a client a couple of blocks away. I saw you from across the street."

She stared at him for a moment, searching for words. "It's beginning to feel like you're stalking me."

"I would hope I'd be a little more subtle if that were the case," he said, unruffled.

She quickly lowered the trunk lid.

Just then, Arthur Hughes came out of the store and trotted down the sidewalk, waving wildly, his lime-green shirt waging a color assault with his neon-orange pants. "Audrey, you princess! I just sold the last of your pots yesterday. Your timing could not be better!"

"Hi, Arthur," she said, anxious now for Nicholas to leave.

"I saw you pull up. I was on the phone, or I'd have been out sooner to give you a hand. Um, hello," he said, looking at Nicholas with ill-concealed appreciation.

Nicholas nodded politely.

"Since Audrey's not going to bother with introductions—" Arthur aimed a playful swat her way "—I'll be so bold. Arthur Hughes. I'm the proprietor. City Gardener," he said, pointing back at the store. "Incidentally selling the hound out of Audrey's lovely pots. Maybe I could interest you in one?"

"Ah, no," Audrey said. "Mr. Wakefield really has to go."

"Actually, I have a few minutes," Nicholas said, glancing at his watch and then meeting Audrey's gaze. "I'd love to take a look."

"Well, let's get those pots out, Audrey," Arthur said. "We might have a sale on the spot."

"I really don't think—" she began.

"Don't be silly," Arthur argued, stepping in between her and the car. "Modesty won't get us new customers."

Before she could think of a single reasonable

protest, Arthur had pulled one of the pots from the trunk and torn off the newspaper. "Oh, Audrey," he said. "This one is lovely. Maybe your best yet. What do you think, Mr. Wakefield? Doesn't she have a divine sense of color?"

Audrey couldn't bring herself to look at Nicholas. She pressed her lips together and folded her arms across her chest, hearing Jonathan's derisive tone in a reply that had not yet been given.

"Did you paint this?" Nicholas asked.

"Yes," she said, groping for some way, any way to make him change his mind and leave.

"It's beautiful."

She looked up at him then and saw the respectful appreciation in his eyes. She tried to respond, but couldn't find her voice.

"So you're an artist?"

No one had ever called her that. She'd never thought of herself that way. It seemed like a word for someone who had plans and ambitions, and all of hers had long ago ceased to exist. "No," she said. "It's just a hobby."

"Well, if it is, it's becoming a profitable one," Arthur interjected. "I have orders for at least six of the pots you brought today."

Unsettled, Audrey reached inside the trunk and lifted one out. "We'd better get these unloaded. I have somewhere else to be."

Nicholas glanced at his watch. "And I have to go. Nice to meet you, Arthur. Bye, Audrey."

She raised a hand, then turned her back as he walked away.

"Lucky thing, you," Arthur said, staring after Nicholas. He gave himself a shake, then picked up a pot. "Ah, well. So what's your connection with that lovely man?"

Audrey shook her head. "There isn't one."

Arthur put a hand on his hip. "Hah. I've been wrong about a lot of things in my life. Trust me. I'm not wrong about the current zinging back and forth between you two. Now come inside before some customer runs off with the contents of my register. Are we doing cash today, same as usual?"

"Please," Audrey said. "Cash would be great."

THE MEETING was a waste of time.

Nicholas sat at a large round table with the board of directors from one of the city's largest banks and tried to focus on what they were saying. But his thoughts were elsewhere. Questions filled his mind with little hope of any answers.

He thought about what Kyle had said the night before. Did he know what he was getting into?

He kept seeing Audrey's face, that pleased look in her eyes when he had complimented her work.

The gratitude that someone had noticed, quickly replaced by alarm, as if he had discovered a secret she did not wish to share.

He was beginning to think Audrey Colby had more than a few secrets.

ONCE AUDREY LEFT the City Gardener, she drove to a mall at the north end of Atlanta and repeated her shopping spree with different credit cards.

She arrived home at just after one o'clock, and the phone was ringing when she walked in the door. Caller ID flashed Blocked Call. Jonathan's cell number was blocked. She picked it up, said hello, trying not to sound as if she'd just run in the house.

"Audrey. It's Nicholas. Please, don't hang up."

She stood for a moment, too startled by the sound of his voice to respond.

"Audrey?"

"Yes?" she said, attempting to instill something remotely close to composure in her voice.

"Can you meet me somewhere?"

Again, surprise robbed her of an immediate answer. She drew in a deep breath, curling her fingers into a fist to keep her hands from shaking. "You have no idea what you're doing."

"That I can't disagree with. But all the same, will you meet me?"

"I can't."

"Then I'll come there."

"No! No."

"If you won't agree to see me somewhere else, I won't have a choice."

His tone left little doubt that he meant it. She could not risk him coming to the house again. Not today. Tomorrow, her whole life was going to change. She couldn't do anything to risk this plan. It felt too much like her last chance. "All right," she said. "All right. Where?"

"Nolan Park. Take exit 260 off the Interstate. Right at the light and then two miles down. There'll be a sign on your left. I'll meet you there in thirty minutes."

And before she could say another word, he hung up.

IT WAS ONE OF those midwinter afternoons warm enough to imply that spring lurked just around the corner. Fifty-five degrees and sunny. Birds held an early celebration of choral joy for the change in weather.

Nicholas sat on a bench near the park entrance, Lola at his feet. He had driven his own car farther in and walked back to wait for Audrey. His right knee shook up and down in a telltale show of nerves. He looked down at Lola. "She's right," he said. "This *is* insane. What exactly am I going to say to her?"

Lola put her head on her paws and looked the other way.

He hardly needed a dog to confirm his audacity. But throughout the morning, the words from the reports Kyle had shown him banged back and forth in his thoughts like a warning bell growing louder and louder until he could think of nothing else.

Once he'd left the building and made that call to Audrey, the noise in his head quieted.

Out on the main road, a black BMW turned into the park. Nicholas stood, his heart kicking hard against his chest. Lola followed him, staying close to his side.

Audrey spotted him and stopped. He crossed the road. She lowered her window, and at the sight of her, a growing web of attraction caught and held him. "Park here, and we'll walk?"

Without acknowledging his words, she pulled into a space and cut the engine. She got out quickly, walking fast and furious down a concrete path marked with a sign that said Nature Trail.

Nicholas followed her.

She went straight into the woods, not slowing until they were well away from the road with nothing around them but trees.

She stopped suddenly and whirled on him. "Is this what you do for fun? Target married women who are absolutely no threat to your bachelor-hood?" Her voice wavered with anger.

"Is that what you think?"

"I have no idea what to think."

He waved a hand at one of the nearby benches. "Can we sit down?"

She stared at him for several moments, then went over to the bench and sat on one end. He took a spot a couple of feet away from her. Lola lay on the ground between them.

The park felt deserted, the only sounds the chirp of a squirrel, the rustle of dry leaves scattering under a cool breeze. They might have been the only two people within miles.

Audrey glanced down at the dog. Something in her face softened. "Is she yours?"

"Yes," he said. "Lola."

She was silent for a moment, and then said, "You don't strike me as the kind of man to have a dog."

He leaned forward, one elbow on his knee. "I didn't strike myself that way not so long ago."

She pressed her lips together, as if she refused to ask anything personal about him.

"She sort of found me," he offered anyway.

Audrey reached down and rubbed the back of her hand under the dog's chin, the tightness around her mouth softening. Lola lifted her head, her eyes closed. It was the first time Nicholas had seen her not shy from the touch of someone she didn't know.

Audrey rubbed behind Lola's ear, then pulled her hand away and tucked it under the other in her lap.

"I cannot afford to be anything other than straightforward with you," she said, her voice low and urgent. "So let me be clear about this. You have no idea what you are jeopardizing."

The anger he had felt emanating from her a few minutes ago had disappeared. Her voice held something different now, something closer to desperation. And he wondered what kind of man he was to put her in this position. "I thought you might need a friend, Audrey. That's all."

She shook her head. "I want you to leave me alone."

He slid down the bench until mere inches separated them.

She looked at him then, and the pain in her eyes squeezed all the air from his lungs.

He felt removed from himself, as if something else were directing him. His gaze locked on hers, he reached out and brushed her cheek with the back of his hand. Her lips parted, and she made a small sound of surprise.

His hand dropped lower to the collar of her blouse. He pushed it aside, keeping his touch gentle. The bruise had faded to a dull yellow. "He hurts you, doesn't he?"

Audrey drew in a sharp breath, reached up to push him away. But his hand covered hers. "Doesn't he?" His voice was soft but insistent.

She stood abruptly, putting distance between them. "Why are you doing this?"

He shrugged. "I don't know. I don't seem to have a choice. I can't stop thinking about you. I imagine what might be—"

"Don't," she said quickly. "Don't."

He closed the gap between them, stood close enough now that he could smell the sweet scent of her perfume. "Let me help you, Audrey."

Her green eyes were wide and glistening with sudden tears. "You can't help me, Nicholas. You can't."

He sensed that was as close to an admission of need as he was going to get. And it reinforced his determination to make her see that he *could* help. Something vital in him depended on it. "Audrey. The last thing I want is to presume to know anything about your life. But I've seen enough bad stuff to make it hard to look the other way."

She folded her arms across her chest, as if trying physically to hold herself together. "I have to go. Please don't call me again, Nicholas."

She turned to walk away, and he was overcome

with an almost desperate need to make her listen. Lola stood, whined once and looked up at Nicholas.

"Not one of the women whose name came across my desk ever thought it would happen to them," he said, his voice thick with urgency.

Audrey stopped, her back to him.

He didn't wait for her response but plunged on, the words pouring out of him now.

"Ashley Arrington. Twenty-three years old. Stabbed to death in her living room. Her three young children also murdered. Ashley's husband, the kids' stepfather, was charged with the crime. He's never been apprehended."

Audrey stiffened, but she did not move. The breeze lifted her hair from her shoulders. Nicholas moved a few steps closer.

"Betty Howell. Forty-five years old. Her husband hit her over the head with a beer bottle because she failed to have his dinner ready when he got home from work. He's doing time for involuntary manslaughter. He'll be out in a few years."

Nicholas had not forgotten any of the women whose fate had been captured in single snapshots, the final outcome of the abusive relationships in which they had been trapped. Somehow, he had to make Audrey see how easily she could become one of them. He forced himself to go on, hoping his words might save her from that same fate.

"Lori Sigmon. Thirty-four. Her husband shot her in the back as she tried to run from the house with their two-year-old daughter.

"Arlene Smith. Twenty-nine. She's been in a coma for four years since her husband beat her so badly her parents could barely identify—"

"Enough!" Audrey swung around then, one hand raised against the onslaught of his words. "Please. No more. No more."

Tears streamed from her eyes. Nicholas's heart turned over, and he cursed himself for causing her more pain. He walked toward her, stopping a few inches away, and shoved his hands in his pockets because that was the only way he could keep from touching her. "I know what hopeless feels like," he said. "But there's light on the other side if you just let yourself believe you can get to it."

They stood there in the shadows of the winter-bare trees, sunlight dappling through. Lola came and sat next to them. Neither Nicholas nor Audrey spoke. They simply looked at one another. For Nicholas, it was something he had wanted to do from the moment they'd met, take in her beautiful face without having to censor his response. He wanted to kiss her. He couldn't remember a moment in his life when he had felt this kind of attraction to a woman, this kind of need to know her touch.

He reached out then, brushed her lashes with his thumb, felt the moisture there. Her eyes on his, she drew in a short, quick breath, her lips parting.

He leaned in then and kissed her, all his senses suddenly amplified.

He hadn't planned this, and it had the feel of something unexpectedly wonderful, a gift that had no occasion. Her mouth was soft against his, accepting. He felt her surprise and her response as well.

She pulled away as quickly as she had yielded, her eyes wide and startled. She swung a panicky glance in both directions, the back of her hand at her mouth.

"There's no one here," he said.

"You shouldn't have done that."

"I'm sorry."

She started to say something, then pressed her lips together.

"No. That's a lie, Audrey. I'm not sorry. I've wanted to do that since New Year's Eve."

She folded her arms and stared into the distance. "Nicholas, I'm not the woman for this."

He put a hand on her shoulder, turning her to face him. "I can't explain it to myself, but from the moment I met you, there was this feeling of inevitability, like it was supposed to have happened all along. And I didn't know it before, but I knew it then. The more I try to forget about you, the more I can't think about anything else."

He could see her weighing his words. The acceptance of truth meant trust. What could be less possible for a woman whose life was controlled by a man who had promised to protect her and broken that promise?

But something in her eyes told him that she wanted to believe him. She dropped her gaze. "This can't happen, Nicholas. You have to understand that."

He reached out, tipped her chin up, forcing her to look at him. "I saw the reports for the domestic disturbance calls at your home. Why did you refuse to press charges against Jonathan?"

"Is that how the report read?" she asked, something long-resigned in her expression.

"How should it have read?"

She shook her head. "It doesn't matter now."

"It matters."

She just stood there, quiet.

"Let me help you, Audrey."

She bent down to rub the side of Lola's face, straightening, she said, "Another woman. Another life." She turned then and walked away.

CHAPTER TEN

THE DRIVE BACK to Buckhead passed in a blur.

She drove too fast. She recognized her reckless-ness and yet needed to put miles between her and what had happened in that park with Nicholas.

Had she lost her mind?

She had driven out there to tell him in no un-certain terms to leave her alone, anger propelling her the entire way. She wasn't sure what she had expected, but it wasn't the man she found waiting for her there.

She hadn't been prepared for his kindness.

Or his kiss. And for the first time in so long, she thought about herself. About her own needs and how insanely wonderful that kiss had felt.

She pressed her hand to her mouth. The feel-ing lingered, settled in, touched places inside her long frozen.

There had been moments in the past few years when she felt as if she had become an emotional robot, getting through each day by never allowing herself the luxury of examining her own wants and needs. She had simply let them flicker out, like the light of a dying candle.

And yet she could not deny that his touch tapped a tiny chink in the armor she had built around herself, allowing feeling, lovely and unexpected, to seep inside.

For a moment, she acknowledged its existence, let it flow through her, warm and real. She imagined being a different woman who might respond to those feelings, acknowledge the attraction.

But it could be nothing more than imagination. It would never happen again. Because today was the last time she would ever see him.

ONCE AUDREY LEFT, Nicholas walked back to his car, let Lola in the passenger seat, then got in the driver's side and sat staring at the steering wheel, thinking of the people he'd failed in his life. Mary-Ellen Moore. His parents. His sister.

Was this what drew him to Audrey Colby? A chance at redemption? A chance to right at least one of the wrongs in this world?

On some level, maybe so.

But there was more. He'd be lying to himself to pretend otherwise.

He felt a dozen different things when he looked at her. Beneath the surface layers of sympathy and fear for her safety was something he'd never felt before. A tangle of emotions that made him wish they had met a long time ago.

Another woman. Another life. Her words. Was that the final answer then?

He reached for his keys, started the car, and pulled out of the parking lot.

Maybe it should be.

But somehow, he knew it wasn't.

NOTHING ABOUT Friday morning distinguished it from any other morning when Jonathan left for a business trip, usually to look at some potential development property. Audrey didn't ask his reason for going to the Dominican Republic. It didn't matter to her why he was going. Only that he was.

His alarm went off at four, and Audrey lay in bed listening to the sound of the shower, eyes wide open, heart pounding. She had not slept the entire night, aware of every breath he drew, counting each as one closer to the morning.

His flight was scheduled to leave at 7:00 a.m. Jonathan hated to be late. He would leave the house by 4:45, allowing plenty of time for the unexpected.

The bathroom light flicked off. He crossed the bedroom floor, stopping at her side of the bed. "Audrey?"

"Hmm?" She raised her head, squinting as if she had been asleep.

"I'm leaving."

"All right," she said.

"I've asked Ross to stop and check on you and Samuel each day. He has my numbers in case he needs to get in touch with me."

Audrey heard the unspoken warning behind the words.

"He doesn't need to do that," she said, as if Jonathan had made his arrangements out of the care and concern a normal husband might have exhibited at leaving his wife alone for five days.

"I left my itinerary on the kitchen table. Except for today and Tuesday, you should be able to get me at those numbers."

She nodded, not trusting herself to speak, afraid that something in her voice might make him suspicious, might change his mind about going. And that was unthinkable.

He bent down to kiss her on the forehead. "See you on Tuesday."

"All right." She pulled the covers up around her as if she intended to go back to sleep.

He left the room, and she lay there, staring into the darkness, listening for the whir of the garage door, the sound of Jonathan's car backing out and then driving away.

For the next forty-five minutes, she forced herself to stay in bed just in case he came back for something. Each minute seemed like a week. She waited until the alarm clock on the nightstand flipped forward to five-thirty, and then she got up and began to pack.

THEY WERE FLYING first-class.

Laura adjusted the angle of her seat back and glanced at the man beside her.

She couldn't believe she was actually here. That he had asked her to go. Or that she'd ditched school for a week to come.

But how could she not? It was exactly what she yearned for. A chunk of time with him that was hers and hers alone.

She wondered what her father would say if he found out. Since her early teenage years, this was the question that prefaced most of her actions. Certainly, all of the rebellious ones. Laura loved getting away with behavior she knew her father would disapprove of.

She considered it payback for all the times he had disappointed her.

And there had been many.

The clink of dishes sounded from the galley where the stewardess was putting together the morning meal. Across the aisle from them an older couple chatted about the excursions they planned to take upon reaching the Dominican Republic.

Jonathan tapped a few keys on his laptop, stared at the screen, his jaw tight in the way that meant he was giving something his full consideration.

He looked up and met her gaze.

She let him see her hunger, uncensored by the games she normally felt obligated to play with him.

He lifted her blanket, put his hand on her leg and stroked her thigh for a few blood-warming seconds.

The stewardess stuck her head around the galley door. "Would you like coffee or tea, Mr. Colby?"

"Coffee," he said, his voice smooth as melted chocolate.

"And you?" she asked Laura.

"Tea, please," she said, her response slightly fractured.

The stewardess disappeared behind the curtain again.

Jonathan picked up where they'd left off a few moments before.

Laura closed her eyes and wondered what her father would have said about that.

NICHOLAS BURIED HIMSELF in work on Friday, a valiant but wasted effort to crowd Audrey out of his thoughts.

He couldn't quit thinking about her.

Or that kiss in the park yesterday.

He'd relived it a hundred times. The softness of her cheek beneath his hand. The surprise he'd felt when she kissed him back.

Let it go. Let *her* go. Forget you ever met her.

The refrain beat a steady drum in his head, and yet her hold on him was complete. He could no more resist the pull than an ocean tide could resist the moon.

AFTER WORK, he found himself in his car, headed toward Buckhead without a clue what he planned to say to her. But the need to see her had a force of its own, lifting him outside the boundaries of common sense and reason.

He pulled into the driveway, got out and followed the stone walkway to the front door. A newspaper lay at the foot of the steps. He picked it up and rang the bell.

No answer. He rang it again and waited a full five minutes. He dropped the paper on the step and walked around the corner of the house to see if anyone was in the backyard. No one there. He walked by the garage, and feeling like an intruder, peered through one of the windows running the width of the door. Both cars were gone.

She could be anywhere. Visiting family. Staying overnight with a friend. But something didn't feel right.

He got back in his car and sat there staring at the house.

You have no idea what you're jeopardizing.

The words came back to him with a crack, like lightning striking right beside his ear.

Audrey wasn't here. And she wasn't coming back.

There was nothing logical about how he knew. He just did.

He sat there for a long time, letting himself absorb the possibility. If she had found a way out, then wasn't that for the best? He'd seen guys like Jonathan Colby come through the system countless times. They never let go. Never. Her only hope would be to start over somewhere else. A place where Jonathan couldn't find her.

That would be the right thing for Audrey. And maybe for him, too. If she had left for good, then he would have no choice but to forget her.

Why then did he feel this awful sense of mourning? Of loss. As if he'd just lost something that might have changed his life?

THE PLANE LANDED at London's Heathrow just before seven on Saturday morning.

Since they were traveling under their real passports, the packet of tickets Audrey had received included a set of instructions that would lead them first to Zurich. From there, they would catch a train, changing a number of times before they eventually ended up in Italy. Once in Europe, she was to pay for everything with cash, thereby not leaving a trail of credit-card purchases to be followed.

Sammy sat in the window seat, Audrey next to him, her hand clasped tightly with his.

"Is that London, Mama?"

"Um-hm. Kind of hard to see with all that fog, isn't it?"

"Is it always like that here?"

"Not always, no."

"Is this where we're staying?"

"Just for a few hours."

"And then we have to go back home?"

"No, honey," she said, touching his face. "Then we're going on another airplane."

"We're going to live somewhere different now?"

"Yes, somewhere very different." They had played this game all the way across the Atlantic, Sammy asking the same questions in a slightly different form as if he couldn't quite believe she was telling him the truth. And how could she blame him? She had tried before and failed.

Sammy looked up at her. "It sounds nice."

His sad, disbelieving smile tied a knot in her heart.

THEY HAD a six-hour layover at Heathrow. Audrey was nearly sick with nerves. The thought of food was unbearable, but Sammy needed to eat. The airport had an enormous shopping area with a McDonald's, Sammy's favorite.

He plucked at his fingers, worry wrinkling his small forehead. "Are you sure it's okay, Mama?"

Jonathan had forbidden her to take him to McDonald's or any other fast-food chain, his reasoning, Audrey suspected, more about denying Sammy something he enjoyed than keeping him away from food that might not be good for him. "More than okay. In fact, bet I can eat more French fries than you can."

"Bet you can't," he said and giggled.

WHEN THEY FINALLY boarded the plane at one that afternoon, relief pummeled through Audrey, leaving her limp with exhaustion. Sammy was already asleep with his head on her shoulder. She leaned back and closed her eyes in silent prayer. *Please, God, be with us. Guide us to this new home. Please don't let me disappoint my son again.*

She had said the words a hundred times in the

past twenty-four hours until it felt as though they were on automatic repeat.

Logic told her not to worry. Even if Ross had already reported back to Jonathan that Audrey wasn't at home, there was little he could do about it from the Dominican Republic. She had the advantage of a head start.

But it wasn't until they had landed in Switzerland three hours later, gathered their luggage and boarded the train that Audrey let the smallest flicker of hope come to life. It pushed up inside her like daffodils through a spring snow, insisting on existence.

For Sammy, she had struggled to look confident, sure of this plan. She had spent the past five months scraping up money from every source she could find, defining each step of her escape and then going over and over its weaknesses, looking for anything that might cause it to fail.

From the moment they had driven away from the house, Sammy had never asked the first question about why they were leaving. This in itself was enough to tell her she had done the right thing. That she should have somehow managed to do it sooner.

THE JOURNEY GREW more grueling each time they switched trains. Sammy was exhausted. Audrey could see it in the droop of his small shoulders, the heaviness of his eyes. But he never complained, and she knew that he wouldn't. If possible, the depth of her desire to protect him deepened, became even more fierce, pulled her on when she herself felt as if she could drop to her knees and sleep for a week.

In Innsbruck, Austria, they changed trains again, the length of the trip from here to Rome allowing them time to sleep. Audrey had purchased a ticket for a sleeper car, and she saw the visible relief on Sammy's face when they stepped inside to find two bunk beds waiting for them.

"Top or bottom?" she asked, smiling at him.

"Can I have the top?"

"Absolutely." She unpacked his pajamas and helped him out of his clothes. He climbed up the narrow ladder. She tucked the covers around him, kissed his cheek and said, "I love you."

But his eyes were already closed, and he was fast asleep.

AUDREY DIDN'T BOTHER to take off her own clothes. She lay down on her bed and fell asleep as quickly as Sammy had, as if she had lapsed into a coma, exhaustion finally getting the best of her.

She awoke to the awful sense that something was wrong.

She sat straight up, her heart pounding with such

sudden fierceness that she felt dizzy. Light trickled through the cabin curtain, announcing daybreak.

She sent a frantic glance around the room, got up and checked on Sammy. He was asleep. She tested the lock on the door and stuck her head inside the small bathroom. Everything was fine. They were safe.

Audrey stood in front of the sink, turned on the water, wet a washcloth and held it to her face. Was this how it would be for the rest of her life? Terror lurking behind every closed door?

She could not do that to Sammy. They were starting over. She would go on as if the past was gone. Over. She could not look back. Because if she did, how would she ever make Sammy believe that he was safe? That peace would be a way of life for them both from now on?

She thought of all the things they had left behind. Her parents. Sammy's friends. His school, what little stability there had been in his young life.

And she thought of Nicholas. Of those few moments in the park when he had kissed her, and she had wanted something for herself.

She put down the washcloth and stared at her reflection in the cloudy cabin mirror. She touched a hand to her lips, remembering the feel of his mouth against hers.

She dropped her hand to her side. Those feelings had no place in her life now. Nicholas could have no way of knowing that. He had simply picked the wrong woman. What had existed between them had never passed the stage of possibility, but she had left that behind, too, selfish though it seemed.

SAMMY AWOKE to an unfamiliar sound.

He opened his eyes wide, straining to see in the darkness. His heart pounded in his chest, so fast he could feel its flutter in his throat. He was breathing too hard, as if he'd just run all the way around the track at his school.

He listened to the strange chug-a-chug-a-chug. Remembered then that they were on a train. He closed his eyes.

He was used to waking up scared and hearing noises he didn't understand at first—then realizing they were awful things he wished he hadn't heard. Wished he could pretend were just a bad dream.

But his mom said they were going to make a new life in another place.

Would it work this time?

Or would they end up going back like before?

He lay there in the dark, his heart settling. Sammy wished his family were like other families. Wished he had a father who thought the little things he did were a big deal. His friend Bobby had a family like that. Bobby talked about his daddy all the time. About how he took him fishing on the weekend. Or skiing in the wintertime.

Sammy wondered what he'd done wrong. For a long time, he'd tried to be perfect. To do everything exactly how he was supposed to. But he didn't think his daddy even noticed. And it didn't make him any less mad at him.

He knew his father was mostly mad at his mama. But he couldn't remember one time when he had told him he was good at something. Or even smiled at him.

Sammy used to love his father. Thought he was some kind of hero. People looked at him with respect on their faces. He used to think it was because he was so successful and smart.

But he understood now that it was because he was one of those people who got their way no matter what.

Sammy never wanted to be like that.

He stuck his head over the side to make sure his mom was sleeping below him. He settled back in his bunk, staring at the ceiling. Now that he remembered where they were, the train's sound was nice. The quiet chug-a-chug made his eyes feel heavy and gritty. He wanted to sleep. But he was afraid if he let himself, he'd wake up to find it was

all a dream. That they weren't really going somewhere different. Making a new life.

Just the words made him happy. The hope he'd
been trying to hold back since his mom had
driven them away from their house that morning
filled his chest.

He never wanted to see his dad again.

THEY CHANGED TRAINS in Rome.

They were in a regular passenger car this time,
Sammy by the window, the eagerness in his little-
boy face making Audrey ache with love. She sensed
the difference in him already, his young heart so
willing to accept that life could change this quickly,
that the bad could be left behind with only good
ahead. She prayed that she would not let him down.

"Look, Mama," he said. "What kind of trees are
those on that hill?"

"Olives," she said.

"They look old."

"I imagine they are. When their leaves come
back, they're a really pretty silver-green."

"Do they taste like regular olives?"

"Probably better."

A few minutes away from their stop, the train
began to slow. Audrey's stomach tightened, as it
had each time they'd approached a new place, and
she'd envisioned Jonathan waiting to drag them

off. The train continued to slow until it arrived at the station with a muted whoosh-whoosh.

"Firenze." The conductor made the announcement. The doors opened.

"Are we there, Mama?"

"Yes, honey, we're here."

She could see in Sammy's face that the words were as meaningful to him as they were to her.

A CAR HAD BEEN RESERVED for them at the train station. Sammy asked if they could get a red one. Red it was, and so small that even their meager luggage engulfed the whole of the back seat.

"It's like a toy," Sammy said, his face lit up. "I bet I could drive this."

Audrey smiled and unfolded the map that had been included with their tickets. She had been nervous about this part, navigating them out of the city, and so she had spent part of the flight studying the layout of Florence until the streets and directions made sense to her. She handed it to Sammy. "Will you be the map holder?"

"Okay," he said, beaming a little as he folded it so the highlighted path was clearly visible.

And then they were off, pulling out of the parking lot of the train station into the midday traffic, cars all around squeezed shoulder to shoulder on the narrow streets, vying for position.

The old fears simmered beneath the surface, and she knew it would be a long, long time before either of them could hear a door slam without jumping, a loud voice without flinching. If ever.

What Audrey yearned for more than anything in the world was peace. For life to be made up of simple things, simple emotions. Smiles and laughter, both free of the censorship caused by someone else's unreasonable jealousy.

The weight that had sat on her chest since the beginning of this journey suddenly felt lighter, and it didn't feel so difficult to breathe. Maybe deep down, she hadn't been willing to let herself believe this could actually work, that she and Sammy could end up in a place where Jonathan would not find them. And now relief floated up from within her like a hot-air balloon released from its tether.

The city of Florence was as breathtaking as she had imagined it might be, with so many things to look at it was difficult to keep her eyes on the road. The Autostrada Del Sole sign popped up on their right. Audrey merged into the traffic, then settled into the right-hand lane, intent on staying there. Cars whizzed by on their left, their colors little more than a blur. They followed the road for several kilometers until they reached the exit for the Superstrada, watching for signs to Certaldo.

Once they exited, the roads narrowed, winding

through the Tuscan countryside with enough hooks and angles that Audrey barely pushed the car out of third gear. Livestock munched hay in very small, neatly fenced pastures, the grass nearly nonexistent. Grapevines lined the slopes beside every home they passed.

The countryside was incredibly beautiful, as if they had stepped into an old painting, the colors rich and muted.

It was late afternoon when she finally spotted the name of the road on her directions. They bumped along for ten minutes or so, counting right-hand turns until they reached the fifth. This was it.

Audrey's heart began to pound, but she forced a confident smile for Sammy. "We're here."

He sat up in his seat, peering over the dashboard, his little face caught between eagerness and fear. Audrey felt the same. What if something wasn't as she'd thought? She'd put her trust in a woman she had never met, whom she had communicated with only by e-mail. Suddenly, the whole plan felt insane.

A farmhouse came into sight at the end of the road. Washed old stucco walls, faded green shutters attached to casement windows that could be thrown open in warm weather, a clay-tile roof, faded and worn. The small yard was made up of more bare spots than grass. A half-dozen chickens pecked away to the right of the house. The scene was worlds removed from the life they had just left behind. And Audrey had never seen anything more wonderful.

A woman appeared from the back of the house, smiling and waving. They got out of the car.

"Audrey?" the woman asked.

"Yes."

"And you must be Sammy."

Sammy nodded and slipped his hand inside Audrey's. She gave it a reassuring squeeze.

"I'm Celine Thomas," she said. "Please call me Celine. I'm so glad you're here. You must be exhausted."

She was American, and younger than Audrey had expected, fortyish, with shoulder-length brown hair tucked behind her ears. Her features were not extraordinary, her nose small, her lips thin. But there was something about her that drew a second glance; a look in her eyes, that said she had seen a lot of things in her life.

She led them toward the house. They followed her to the front steps where she pulled a key from her pocket and opened the door. The walls were a terra-cotta stucco, the floors worn tile. The house had a rustic warmth to it that made Audrey limp with appreciation. Nothing had ever looked more welcoming.

On the kitchen table were two loaves of bread,

freshly made if the smell were an indication, a bottle of red wine, a bowl of fruit. There was a pot on the stove, and it smelled of sage and onion.

"I thought you might be hungry," Celine said. "The beds have fresh linens, and there are towels in the bathroom. Oh, and there's bottled water in the pantry."

"Thank you," Audrey said, her voice wavering as tears welled up.

Celine reached out to squeeze Audrey's hand. "I know how you feel. And really, I'm so glad you're here."

"I don't know what to say. This is more than I ever—"

"I know. I've been in your shoes," she said quietly. "You can stay here as long as you want."

"I'll pay you rent, of course."

"Don't worry about any of that right now. Just focus on the fact that you're safe." And with that, she slipped out the door and left them alone in their new home.

AUDREY AND SAMMY ate the wonderful food Celine had made for them, then put on their pajamas and got into bed, even though it wasn't yet dark. Sensing that he needed her nearby, Audrey slid into bed beside him, pulling him close and breathing in his sweet little-boy smell.

He fell asleep immediately, and she lay there in the twilight, thankful. They had made it. For so long, she had hoped and planned, prayed and feared.

Lying here in this quiet house with her sleeping son in her arms, Audrey closed her eyes and slept the sleep of the peaceful.

CHAPTER ELEVEN

WHEN ROSS ARRIVED at the office on Monday morning, he looked as if he'd been held under boiling water for twenty-four hours. His face red, he stood in the doorway of Nicholas's office, a rumpled, off-kilter version of himself.

"You haven't heard from Audrey Colby, have you?" he asked.

Nicholas raised an eyebrow, cool, even as his heart kicked up. "Should I have?"

Ross ran a hand through his hair. "No. I just thought...she hasn't been home all weekend. Jonathan had asked me to check in on her. He's calling this morning. I don't know what I'm going to tell him."

"That you don't know where she is?"

Ross lifted a shoulder and looked at Nicholas with narrowed eyes, as if debating how much to say. "Jonathan is a little...protective of Audrey."

"Is that what you call it these days?"

If possible, Ross's face grew redder. "This isn't

kindergarten, Wakefield. Watch your step. He's not a guy you want to mess with."

"Apparently not."

Ross stared at him for a moment, then swung off, his Cole-Haan lace-ups pounding an angry path back down the hall.

Nicholas crossed the office floor and stood at the window looking out at the morning traffic. He wondered where Audrey had gone, and if he would ever see her again.

THE SOUND of laughter pulled her from sleep.

Audrey sat straight up in bed, disoriented, and looked at the clock on the nightstand. One in the afternoon. Impossible. She'd slept the entire night and half the next day?

She flung herself out of bed and ran to the front door. Sammy was in the yard, flat on his back, an enormous yellow Labrador retriever standing above him, licking his face with every giggle.

Standing guard a few feet away was Celine Thomas. She looked up and spotted Audrey. "Good morning. I mean good afternoon."

"I can't believe I slept this long. Has he been up—"

"Just a few minutes ago. I came down to see if you would like to join me for lunch. I think George has found a new friend."

"I think Sammy has, too," Audrey said, smiling.

"So how about that lunch?" Celine asked.

"Can we go, Mama? Mrs. Thomas says she lives right up that hill. And George lives there with her."

Audrey's eyes met Celine's and she saw the same compassion she had glimpsed there last night. "That sounds wonderful."

"Whenever you're ready," she said, "just follow the path through the trees there. You'll see the house in no time. Come on, George. Let's go."

George trotted off behind her, sending a woeful glance back at Sammy who looked up at Audrey and said, "Can we hurry, Mama?"

"Bet I'll be ready before you," she said, racing for the door.

"No way. You're a girl," he said and flew past her.

CELINE THOMAS'S HOUSE was like something out of a fairy tale.

Audrey and Sammy came to the end of the path and both stopped, staring.

"Wow," Sammy said.

The farmhouse was Tuscan in design, the roof clay tile. The sides were stucco, the windows framed with bold blue shutters. A closer look at the details made it clear the person who lived here had taken pride in making it a home. Window boxes brimmed with herbs and other flowering plants. An enormous painted wood door was flanked by clay pots holding twin juniper trees.

Celine came outside and George stood on the step beside her, wagging his tail. Spotting Sammy, he trotted out to greet them.

"It's nearly two. You must be starving," Celine said. "Come in and let's eat."

The inside of the house was just as interesting, antiques obviously Celine's passion. And the smells coming from the kitchen made Audrey nearly faint with hunger.

Celine led the way to a wonderful old farm table already set with earthenware dishes and bowls of softly steaming food.

"Please, sit," Celine said, indicating a spot for each of them. "George, in your chair, please."

George crossed the room and hopped up in the leather chair that obviously belonged to him.

"This is so nice of you," Audrey said.

"I love to cook," Celine replied. "George there isn't the most discerning of critics. He likes everything."

As it turned out, Celine had been modest about her talent. She was an unbelievable cook, the food simple, but each dish nearly a work of art in its perfection. Roasted chicken with thyme and oregano, crispy potatoes sautéed in olive oil and more of the wonderful bread she had left them last night. For dessert, she brought out slices of chocolate cake that were nothing short of delicious.

"I don't know when I've eaten food that good," Audrey said. "Thank you so much."

"You're welcome." She looked at Sammy. "Would you like to play outside with George for a little while?"

Sammy nodded as if he thought she'd never ask.

"Is it okay?" Celine asked Audrey.

"Of course."

Sammy got up from the table so fast he nearly turned his chair over. "Thank you for the lunch, Mrs. Thomas."

"You're welcome, Sammy. George, go play," she said.

George hopped down and trotted through the kitchen after Sammy. Moments later, playful barks and giggles echoed from the front yard.

"What a delightful child," Celine said.

"Sometimes I don't think I deserve him." The words were out before Audrey realized she intended to say them.

"Espresso?" Celine asked.

"Yes, please."

Celine got up from the table, went over to a black-and-chrome piece of wizardry from which she procured them each a small white cup of rich, dark coffee. She placed Audrey's in front of her, then pulled out a pitcher of cream and set it, along with a bowl of sugar cubes, on the table. Audrey added some of each to hers, then took a sip. "Mmm. Wonderful," she said.

"I've become addicted," Celine said. "Me, a former watery decaf person."

Audrey smiled.

"Back to that comment about not deserving Sammy. Who would deserve him more?"

The question held layers of meaning far beyond what two normal people having met one another for the first time less than twenty-four hours ago should be discussing. But then *normal* wasn't really a word that applied in this case.

When Audrey didn't answer, Celine tucked her hair behind her ears and blew out a sigh. "I never had children. For the very reason you just said. But sometimes I wonder if a child might have given what I went through some meaning. As it is, there is none."

"I would never have chosen to bring Sammy in to the situation," Audrey said.

"I understand." Celine hesitated, studying Audrey's face for a moment. "I know for our own safety, it's wise not to share personal details, but when I saw you get out of that car yesterday, it was like looking back through some kind of mirror and seeing myself as I must have looked three years ago."

"Are you…am I the first woman you've helped?"

"Second."

"Did she come here?"

"Yes. And she went back."

Audrey's stomach dropped. "Oh."

Celine reached across to squeeze her hand. "That doesn't have to be you, Audrey. Walking away from everything you know can get really lonely before it starts to get better. She decided to go back to the devil she knew."

Audrey smoothed her thumb across the rim of her cup. "Do you work?"

"I haven't had to yet. In my previous life, I worked for an investment firm. It's a talent that's come in handy."

"Do you ever get lonely?"

"Sometimes," she said, tilting her head. "At first, it seemed so unfair. That I should have to give up my whole life. But I don't have to tell you that."

"And that part gets better?"

"A little. My stomach still drops when I hear a car coming up the road."

"So you…your husband still doesn't know where you are."

Celine shook her head. "If he did, I wouldn't be alive today."

The words were like ice around Audrey's heart. She might have used them herself.

Celine squeezed her hand again. "I'm sorry. I didn't mean to deepen your worries. Having said what I just said, you're safe here, Audrey."

Audrey nodded and prayed there was no loose end Jonathan might find to unravel this new existence.

"You know, Audrey, we're two people who have been changed forever," Celine said, her voice resigned. "We'll never know what kind of person we might have been, because our experience has reshaped us. But in these last few years, I've tried to figure out who I am, what I can be from here."

"Do you like that person?" Audrey asked the question with trepidation for the answer. Would she ever feel anything close to respect for herself again? It did not seem possible.

"More and more," Celine said. "The important part is to believe that one day you're going to feel the same way."

Tears slipped down Audrey's cheeks. Sitting here across from a woman for whom this was obviously true, she could actually believe it might happen for her as well.

As SOON AS she walked into the room, Laura felt the change in atmosphere.

She had been at the pool. It was nearly noon, and Jonathan had said he would meet her there over an hour ago.

Impatient, she'd decided to come back to see what was keeping him. He'd promised there would be very little work during this trip, that the two of them would have plenty of time together. She intended to hold him to it.

All the curtains were drawn, and he was sitting in a chair by the window, one hand on the telephone.

The look on his face made her breath catch in her throat. Something unfamiliar fluttered in her stomach. "Hey," she said. "Thought you were coming out."

He didn't answer, and she found herself floundering, suddenly unsure.

Something menacing in his manner, he stood, anchoring both palms on the round table next to the chair.

She considered leaving, but pushed aside the fleeting impulse as silly. Less than two hours ago, they'd had sex on the still unmade bed, the rowdy, out-of-breath kind that made her think she would never find another man like him.

She crossed the room and pressed her hand to the center of his back. "What is it, Jonathan?"

Several seconds passed before he answered.

"Your father called. It appears no one seems to know where Audrey is."

She frowned, suddenly hopeful. "What do you mean?"

"I mean that she's gone. That she's left me."

"But how do you know—"

"I know."

Laura hesitated. She caught her lower lip between her teeth and continued to rub his back with the heel of her hand. She considered saying nothing. But she'd been quiet all this time. Maybe this was the opening she'd been waiting for. "I can't say I'm unhappy about that."

He whirled. The strike came so quickly that she was completely unprepared for the force behind it. The back of his hand connected with her jaw, whipped her head sideways. She heard something pop and wondered in a moment of dazed disbelief if he had broken her neck.

Her mouth locked in an O of surprise. She stumbled backward, fell onto the bed, facedown. She could still smell their scent on the sheets.

She lay there, stunned.

She heard him cross the room, open the door and leave without saying a word.

SHE WASN'T SURE how long she stayed in that same position. An hour. Maybe more.

When she finally got up, she did so tentatively.

She walked to the bathroom, one hand on the wall to steady herself.

She raised her gaze to the mirror and gasped.

The left side of her face looked as if it had been injected with air, its shape distorted, grotesque.

She stared at the instant bruise with a kind of detached disbelief. And wondered what her father would have said about that.

AT JUST AFTER six o'clock, Nicholas had reached the tail-end of a thirty-minute phone call with another of Ross's glad-to-hand-this-one-over-to-you clients.

Jonathan Colby walked through the open office door, then flipped it closed. "Hang up," he said.

"Can I call you back, Hank?" Nicholas put the phone on its base, slid back his chair and stood. "Is there something I can help you with, Jonathan?"

"You tell me," he said, arms folded across his chest, his tone low and even. "Is there?"

The threat in the other man's voice had all the subtlety of a Louisiana thunderstorm. "Somehow I feel as if I'm supposed to know what we're talking about."

Jonathan crossed the floor, gripped the edge of the desk with both hands until his knuckles turned white. He leaned in, his face less than a foot from Nicholas's. "Where is my wife?"

The question sounded so normal, the words little more than a whisper. "How would I know?"

"Oh, I think you know."

"I have no idea what you're getting at, but you're way off base."

"Am I?" Jonathan stepped back, his eyes cold.

"Yeah, you are."

"You'd be wise to stay away from her, Wakefield."

Nicholas stared back. "Is that a threat?"

"Call it what you like. But if I ever find out that you had anything to do with Audrey's disappearance, you'll be the one wanting to disappear." Jonathan turned and walked to the door. He stopped and without looking back, said, "I will find her. Make no mistake. She took my son. She will never get away with that."

Jonathan's footsteps receded down the hall. Fear for Audrey billowed through Nicholas like fire fed with a sudden influx of air.

He moved to the window and waited until he saw Jonathan head for the parking garage at the end of the block. He left his office then and headed straight for Ross's, not bothering to knock on the closed door.

Ross looked up, clearly not surprised by Nicholas's appearance. "Shut the door, will you?"

Nicholas did as he asked, then turned and

shoved his hands in his pockets. "Tell me one thing. How do you live with yourself?"

Ross opened a desk drawer and pulled out a cigar. "Care for one?"

"No."

Ross clipped the end, stuck a lighter to it, then took a heavy pull before exhaling a couple of rings of smoke. "I learned a long time ago that there were some things in this world I could change. Some things I couldn't."

"And exactly where does covering up for a client who beats his wife fall in that?"

"Under nothing I can do about it." He blew another puff from the cigar and met Nicholas's gaze. "Isn't that why you wanted out of the prosecutor's office? Because you figured out there were some things in this world you couldn't change?"

"Yeah. Before I realized your world was made up of the same kind of thugs. The only difference is they wear Armani and keep you in expense accounts."

The words hit their target. Ross's face hardened. He tapped the edge of the cigar on the glass ashtray next to his telephone. "Whatever you say."

"How could you look at her knowing what you know?"

Ross laughed, the sound harsh at the edges. "Come on, Nicholas. Don't you think that if she stayed, there must be a reason? She's never wanted for anything."

Nicholas stared at the other attorney. "That's your justification then? How can you take money from a man who holds his wife prisoner in her own life?"

"You don't know what you're talking about."

"Oh, I think I do. I would be willing to bet there was a time when you were a decent man, Ross. When maybe even you imagined locking up guys like Colby. The first time you looked the other way, it tore you up inside, didn't it? But the next time was a little easier. And the next, easier still. And now, you've convinced yourself it doesn't matter. It *does* matter. I'll clean out my desk before I go."

Ross's face bleached of color. "Wakefield, wait—"

But Nicholas walked out without looking back, a sudden certainty quickening his stride. Without a doubt, Jonathan Colby would eventually find Audrey. Guys like Colby never gave up. And one thing was suddenly clear to him. He had to find her first.

ROSS'S PHONE BUZZED thirty seconds after Wakefield left his office. He picked it up, weary. "Yes?"

"Mr. Colby on three."

He could delay the call. Hell, he could take off for Tahiti and leave the whole damn thing behind.

Right. It was way too late for that. He hit the button and put on his most pleasant attorney voice. "Jonathan."

"I want this fixed. I want to know where she is, and I want my son back."

So much for preliminaries. Ross dropped his head against the back of his chair and pressed a thumb against his right temple as if by doing so he might hold back the sudden gush of pain threatening to push through his skull. "What would you like me to do?"

"Put a tail on Wakefield. He doesn't make a move without my knowing where he's going. Got it?"

"Got it." Ross somehow managed to inject a note of confidence in his response, as if he weren't sweating huge stains in the armpits of his Italian-made shirt.

He hung up the phone, feeling as if he might throw up. How he wished he'd never hooked up with the Colby gravy train. Never put himself in the position of cleaning up Colby's dirty laundry.

He pulled a key from his wallet, then opened a side drawer in his desk. He lifted out a batch of files, finding the card he had tucked away there with the detective's number. He stared at it for a moment, then picked up the phone and dialed.

AT JUST AFTER MIDNIGHT, Nicholas drove back downtown and took the elevator to the W&A office suite. Luckily, Ross had not yet announced him as persona non grata to the guard downstairs who waved him by with a friendly smile. His key still worked in the front door as well. He closed the door quietly behind him, then walked to Ross's office. Anything to be found on Colby, Inc., would be there.

A mahogany file cabinet sat behind Ross's chair. The drawers were locked. He ran a hand down the sides, feeling for a key. When he failed to find one, he opened the unlocked drawers, still finding nothing. He ran his hand under the desk and then the bottom of the leather chair.

Bingo.

A small hide-a-key box clung to the metal leg.

There were several small keys inside. He tried each until one fit the file cabinet lock, then pulled it open with a loud click.

He put the key box back in place, then thumbed through the folders until he hit the Cs. Colby, Jonathan. He had his own small library here.

Nicholas glanced at his watch, then flipped through the files quickly. A name caught his eye. Ella Fralin. He yanked the document out of the drawer and rifled through the pages. At the back was a contract. Just like the one he had been working from for the lawsuit she had filed against

Colby, Inc. There were differences, though. He didn't have to read far to see that.

Ross had his own copy machine in the corner of the office. Nicholas turned it on, waited a second or two for it to warm up, then copied the pertinent pages. He returned to the cabinet and stuck the file back in its place.

A janitor stood in the doorway, a vacuum cleaner hose in his hand. "You're here awfully late, Mr. Wakefield."

"Yeah. I just found what I was looking for," Nicholas said, skirting the desk and then walking past the man out into the hall.

HE DIDN'T SLEEP the rest of the night, but instead sat at his kitchen table with a yellow legal pad in front of him. Lola lay at his feet, head on her paws, staring up at him. He felt as if he were starting with less than a blank slate. Audrey could be anywhere in the world. Literally.

Maybe he was crazy to think he could find her. To think that she would want to be found.

But if Nicholas had ever believed anything, he believed Jonathan would exhaust every penny of his not-insignificant wealth to find her. The look in the man's eyes this morning had said it all.

He picked up the pen and began to make a list of every single detail he could remember about Audrey Colby.

THOSE FIRST WEEKS in Certaldo were almost too perfect.

It felt to Audrey as if she and Sammy had been lifted out of their previous life, and, with the lightness of feathers, were drifting back to earth in the hills of Tuscany.

Audrey understood why Celine felt safe here in this valley tucked between hillsides, almost as if the earth itself had wrapped them in its embrace. They were safe here. Safe. It scared Audrey how freely the word came into her thoughts, more so each day.

She felt as if she were standing in the middle of a long highway. To one side was the agonizing fear that Jonathan would somehow track them down. To the other, the peacefulness of security and this quiet existence where she and Sammy took long walks with their lunch in paper bags, and she told him stories at night before he fell asleep snuggled in her arms. They were simple things, but wealth unimaginable to Audrey.

Celine knew someone who could make them new identification papers. They'd used their own passports to get into Italy, but Celine had advised her not to use them now that she was here. As soon as they had their IDs, Audrey planned to enroll Sammy in school.

Celine had a laptop, and Audrey sent an untraceable e-mail to the address she had asked her mother to set up. It was brief and simple, just to let her know that they were all right.

Beginnings were followed by middles, and for Audrey that meant finding a way to support herself. The money she had managed to bring with her would not last forever. It was frightening, in fact, how much of it she had already spent.

She brought the subject up with Celine one unusually warm afternoon in March. Celine had offered to help Audrey clear a patch in her small backyard for a kitchen garden. They were picking up rocks and putting them in the wheelbarrow Celine had brought down earlier.

"I'm going to have to figure out a way to earn some money," Audrey said, moving the wheelbarrow closer to the edge of the plot they'd marked off.

"What did you do before?"

"I never worked after I got married."

"Neither did I. My husband wouldn't allow it."

Audrey nodded, the words hitting a familiar chord, as they had many times between the two of them these past few weeks. Theirs was an unusual friendship, the bond between them immediate and deep. They had fought a similar war, understood each other's scars on a level Audrey knew few people could. "There was something I—" She hesitated. "But it would probably never work here."

Celine stood, pulled off a leather glove and shook some dirt from the inside. "What was it?"

"I painted flower pots and sold them to a kind of high-end retail store."

"How'd they sell?"

"The owner was pleased."

"Then why couldn't you do it here?"

Audrey shrugged. "I don't know. I—"

"Clay pots?"

"Yes."

"We certainly have plenty of those available. What else would you need?"

"Brushes, paint, burnt umber for antiquing."

"We should be able to find all that in San Gimignano. Think you're ready to venture out a bit?"

Just the thought tied Audrey's stomach in knots. She had left the house only twice since their arrival. Once to return the rental car, and again a week or so ago when she and Sammy had gone with Celine to the market for groceries.

Celine had invited them to go on various excursions with her, into San Gimignano, or up to Certaldo Alto, nearby hill towns that under Celine's description sounded fascinating.

"Audrey, I know how you feel," Celine said. "It's terrifying to think of putting yourself out there again. Of risking the safety you've found here. But this is a different world. A new life.

Don't make the mistake of simply creating another prison for yourself and for Sammy. Only you can decide when you're ready, but when you are, let me know."

Audrey nodded, emotion tightening her throat. She glanced across the yard at Sammy, playing fetch with George, his face open and smiling as it had rarely been in his young life. Maybe it was time.

CHAPTER TWELVE

CELINE PICKED THEM UP the next morning at just after nine. George and Sammy were in the back, both sitting as tall as they could to see out the windows of Celine's small car.

"I made a couple of calls last night and found out that there's a man a mile or so from San Gimignano who makes clay pots," Celine said. "You should be able to buy some from him if they're what you're looking for."

Celine's generosity still amazed Audrey. "How will I ever be able to thank you?"

"By becoming the person you want to be. Someone else did the same for me. By helping you, I am repaying them. Maybe one day you'll do the same for someone."

It wasn't anything she would ever have imagined, but even that seemed doable as the day itself overflowed with possibility.

They arrived at the man's house some twenty minutes later. He came out to greet them, his weathered face shaded beneath the brim of a wide straw hat.

Celine spoke to him in Italian, very few words of which Audrey understood. He led them around to the back of the house and the small shop where he made his pots. He waved a hand down an aisle where they were stacked by type.

"He says to pick out what you like," Celine said.

"Thank you." Audrey nodded at the man and walked up and down the various rows, spotting several styles that she loved. She picked out four. "Can you ask him how much these are?"

Celine asked him in Italian and translated back to Audrey. Audrey nodded and said, "I'll take two each of those four."

The man packed the pots up and loaded them into Celine's trunk. And, as they drove away, Audrey began to feel for the first time that she might be regaining control of her life, that she would determine its direction from here on out.

It was a wonderful feeling.

NEARLY SIX WEEKS had gone by, and he had hit dead end after dead end.

He'd spoken to Sammy's teacher and the pastor at Audrey's church. He'd talked to her hairdresser, clerks at the stores where she'd shopped. He went back to the City Gardener and talked to

Arthur Hughes, who had been distressed to learn
that Audrey was gone, but it was clear to Nicholas that the man had no idea why. Nicholas had
even gotten Audrey's maiden name off a document she had signed with Jonathan. After numer-
ous searches through Internet white pages, he had
tracked down her parents, calling their home, only
to be told they had not seen Audrey in a very long
time.

It was as if she had dropped off the face of the
earth.

Since leaving Webster & Associates, Nicholas
had spent his days working on his house, making
a checklist of repair jobs that kept his hands busy,
if not his mind. Lola loved the fact that he was
home most of the time. He could hardly believe
the transformation in her. Where she had once
wilted at the sight of a stranger, she now barked
at the UPS truck, and walked from room to room
with an assurance that her world wasn't going to
fall apart at any second.

He wondered if Audrey had gained the same
kind of security in her new life.

Driving down Piedmont one evening, he
passed the library he'd seen her turn into the afternoon he'd left her house. Farfetched, but worth
a try. At this point, he wasn't above grasping at
straws.

He parked out front, then loped up the front steps to the cool, hushed interior of the library entrance. He walked through the main floor until he found the reference desk. The woman behind the counter was in her fifties with gray hair that looked as if it had been teased with an electric comb. A pair of wire-rimmed oval glasses sat low on her nose. She peered out at him over them. The name badge on her red blazer read Mrs. Olinger.

"May I help you?" she asked.

"I hope so," he said. He reached in his pocket for the photo of Audrey with Jonathan at a fundraiser he'd downloaded from the city newspaper's Web site. "I wondered if you've ever seen this woman."

Mrs. Olinger squinted at the picture, started to shake her head, then looked again. "No. I don't recognize her."

"Are you sure?"

"Yes," she said.

"Is there someone else who works here that I might ask?"

Without answering, she got up from her stool and disappeared behind a door marked Private. A few moments later, another woman approached the desk, eyebrows raised. "Is there something I could help you with?"

He held out the picture. "I wondered if you remember seeing this woman in here."

She took the picture, looked at it for a moment, then handed it back to him. "Is there some reason you're asking?"

"I'm trying to find her. She's…missing."

The woman's eyes widened in surprise. "Oh. And you are?"

"A friend. Nicholas Wakefield."

She studied him for a long moment. "I'm sorry," she said. "I can't help you."

The hope that had begun to build inside him suddenly collapsed. "Are you sure?"

She hesitated and then nodded decisively.

"Thank you anyway," he said, turning and threading his way through the tables scattered throughout the room.

At the elevator, Nicholas pushed the button, then dropped his head back and blew out a sigh. Maybe it was time to give this up, let it go. *Let her go.*

"Mr. Wakefield."

The librarian trotted up, one hand at the neck of her blouse. "Wait," she said. "In general, I don't believe in giving out information about people without their consent. But you seem like a nice man. I do remember her. She asked me a few questions."

"About?" he said, his pulse tripping now.

"MapQuest. She wanted a map of Florence," the woman said. "Florence, Italy."

LAURA'S apartment was in one of the better enclaves of New Haven, not far from the Yale campus.

She lived alone. Roommates were a bore. She'd tried that route a couple of times, decided it wasn't worth the hassle even though her dad balked at the exorbitant monthly rent for the place she'd chosen. He still paid it.

It was almost eight o'clock, and she was beat. She dropped onto the leather sofa in one corner of the living room and flipped on the TV. Jerry Springer rerun. She watched for a moment as a man on the screen picked up a chair and hurled it across the stage. Did people like that actually walk the streets?

She hit Next. *Animal Planet.* Two cougar cubs rolled on the ground, nipping playfully at one another.

The doorbell rang. She glanced at her watch. She wasn't expecting anyone.

She went to the door and peered through the peep hole. Her heart began to pound. "Jonathan. Go away."

"Baby, let me in. I need to talk to you."

She ran a hand under the back of her hair. "What could you possibly have to say?"

"A lot if you would let me."

She hadn't spoken to him since they'd returned from the Dominican Republic. "I don't want to see you," she said. "You shouldn't have come here."

"You won't take my calls. What choice did I have?"

"Go home."

"Laura. I miss you."

She wrapped her arms around her waist, the old attraction igniting against better judgment. Crazy. She'd be crazy to start this up again. But he was like a drug. Out of sight, she could find the will to resist. On the other side of the door, within reach, the temptation was too great.

She put a hand to the side of her face, the bruises long healed. She closed her eyes for a moment, then removed the chain and let him in.

THE EXHILARATION LASTED all the way across the Atlantic. Nicholas landed in Florence just after noon on a Friday. He used a pay phone to call Kyle and check in on Lola. Nicholas had not told Kyle where he was going, but his friend knew him well enough to know it had something to do with Audrey. He assured him that Lola was fine and at that very moment playing in the backyard with the kids.

It wasn't until his feet actually hit the streets of the old city that Nicholas realized the enormity of his undertaking. How did he find someone who didn't want to be found in a population of 400,000?

For the next three days, he walked the streets of Florence until he began to feel like a man possessed. He sat for hours at a small café in the main shopping district, sipping strong coffee, a book on his lap, his heart stopping a little with every blond woman who walked by.

She was here. He could feel it, crazy as it sounded.

On the fourth day, he was up with the sunrise. He pulled on a pair of running pants and a T-shirt, then left the hotel for an early run. The city had just begun to wake up, shopkeepers sweeping the sidewalks in front of their businesses, a few mopeds zipping down empty streets, their drivers steering with one hand, holding cell phones to their ears with the other.

Nicholas ran fast and hard, his shoes hitting the sidewalk with a force his knees would later remind him of. But the pounding was a much-needed outlet for the frustration slowly replacing his hopefulness.

He hung a right and headed down a road whose stores would not open for a few hours. The shops here were mainly aimed at tourists with money to spend. The window cases were backlit, displaying goods for sale, leather-bound photo albums, stylish shoes and coats.

Halfway down the street, something caught his eye. He stopped and backed up, frowning while his memory tugged for recognition.

Two painted pots sat in the corner of the window, their brilliant colors distinctive and familiar. His heart began to pound. They were just like the ones Audrey had sold to the store in downtown Atlanta.

Audrey.

She was here.

He sat down on the window ledge, dropped his head between his knees and waited for his breathing to steady.

She was here.

He glanced at his watch. The shop wouldn't open for another two hours. He would wait.

THE SHOPKEEPER ARRIVED at ten minutes before nine. By that point, Nicholas had nearly worn the soles from his shoes pacing the sidewalk.

The man smiled and nodded, then opened the door and waved him inside.

Nicholas went in and forced himself to browse

the rest of the store before returning to the front
window. "Excuse me."

The man looked up from the cash register. *"Si?"*

"These pots. I would like to buy them."

"Bello, si?"

Nicholas nodded. "Do you have more?"

"No, these are the only ones."

"Will you be getting more?"

"On Friday, I think."

"Are they made locally?"

"Yes. But by an American woman. Also very
beautiful," the man added with a smile.

Nicholas kept his expression casual. "Do you
know what time Friday? I'm not sure how much
longer I will be here."

"She usually comes in the morning. Check with
me around noon."

"Thank you," Nicholas·said. "Thank you."

FOR NICHOLAS, two days seemed longer than a
lifetime. He went to the Uffizi Gallery, the Du-
omo, walked nearly every street in Florence, ran
twice a day from the sheer need to burn energy.

When Friday morning finally arrived, he left his
room at seven and headed back to the little shop,
taking a seat at the café across the street. The store
did not open for two more hours, but he wasn't
taking a chance on missing her. This felt like his

one and only shot; he might very well never have another.

At exactly ten minutes before nine, the shop-keeper arrived and opened his doors. A lady with a small dog stopped and chatted with him while he swept the front sidewalk. The woman lowered her eyes at something the man said, laughed and walked on.

Within the next hour, seven customers came and went. Nicholas ordered another coffee. A small car had pulled up in front of the store, the trunk open. A woman in a straw hat was talking to the shopkeeper who smiled and nodded.

Nicholas glanced back at the car, moving to one side of the café for a better look at the trunk. He spotted the colorful rim of a painted pot.

He set his cup down too fast, the saucer clat-tering against the tabletop, a couple of nearby pat-rons raising curious gazes. Nicholas ignored them, weaving through chairs and hitting the sidewalk at a run without taking his eyes off her.

He crossed the street, a taxi barely missing him, its horn squawking in outrage. At the edge of the sidewalk he forced himself to walk. His hands were shaking, and he could barely get her name out. "Audrey."

She swung around, her smiling face instantly closing.

Not Audrey.

This woman was older with auburn hair visible beneath the front of her hat. A very attractive woman, as the shopkeeper had said. But not Audrey.

"I'm sorry," Nicholas said. "I thought you were…someone else."

The woman put a hand to her heart, started to say something, appeared to struggle for words, then said, "That's all right."

"She is the beautiful lady who brings me the pots," the shopkeeper said, looking puzzled by the interchange. "This gentleman bought the last two," he explained to the woman. "He would like to buy more."

"Yes," Nicholas said. "For gifts."

"Oh," she said, clearing her throat. "How nice. I appreciate it very much."

Disappointment hit Nicholas like a wrecking ball. He had been so sure they were hers. Had it been nothing more than his own wishful thinking? Maybe *he* had gone too far with this. Maybe he was too far gone with it.

The woman walked to the car and lifted out one of the pots. He went around and said, "Let me help you."

As he took the pot from her, he looked down at her hands. They were shaking. He raised his gaze to hers. Her eyes held the same muted turmoil he remembered from before.

She wasn't Audrey.

But she knew where Audrey was.

AUDREY'S DAYS had taken on a routine that gave her life a reassuring sense of structure. She worked each morning from eight until noon in the small shed she had converted into a workshop. Celine had helped her place her pots in three different stores so far, one located in Certaldo Alto and one in San Gimignano. This last shop in Florence had been the most successful yet, and she was hopeful now that she would be able to support Sammy and herself once the rest of her money ran out.

Laughter echoed from the front yard followed by a playful bark. Audrey smiled. She fully believed that the always-ready-to-play George had done more for Sammy in these past weeks than any therapist ever could.

She had no idea how she would ever repay Celine. The other woman had understood Audrey's lingering fear of venturing too far out and had offered to deliver the pots for her until she grew confident enough to do it herself.

Audrey glanced at her watch. Eleven-thirty. Celine was due back any time. They had begun taking long walks each day, and Audrey wasn't sure who enjoyed them more, she and Celine or Sammy and George.

A car rolled down the gravel drive. Audrey no longer jumped at the sound. As trivial as it was, it felt like progress, evidence that one day she might actually live the life of a woman who did not have to look over her shoulder.

A car door slammed. "Sammy, go in the house. Take George with you." Celine's voice held a high, unfamiliar pitch.

Audrey got up, wiped her paint-splotched hands on the apron around her waist. She stepped out of the shed. Celine ran around the side of the house. Her cheeks were flushed, her hair half escaped from the knot at the back of her head.

Something was wrong. "What is it?"

Celine's face crumpled, tears filling her eyes. "A man at the store in Florence. He was looking for you, Audrey. He was looking for you."

AUDREY'S KNEES literally gave way beneath her.

She dropped to the ground, this new existence she had already grown to love crumbling around her.

"Oh, Audrey. I'm so sorry," Celine said. "I should never have suggested taking the pots into Florence."

"It's not your fault." She was still dazed and only just beginning to assimilate what her friend had said. "The man. What did he look like?"

Celine rubbed her arms, regret etched in her expression. "Good-looking. Tall, dark hair."

It could be Jonathan or someone he had sent after her. Either way, she couldn't take a chance. "We have to leave. I should start packing." Even as she said the words, she tried to get up, but her limbs weren't responding. She felt locked up, frozen with shock.

She should have had a backup plan. This had always been a possibility. She had known from the moment she'd left Atlanta. She had just felt so safe here. Allowed herself to believe they would be okay.

"What did you say to him?" she asked.

"I told him he was mistaken."

"Do you think he believed you?"

"I don't know," Celine said, self-blame evident in her tone.

"Did he follow you?"

"I don't think so. He left the store before I did. I'm sorry, Audrey. I was just so caught off guard."

Audrey got up and crossed the short stretch of grass separating them. She took Celine's hand and said, "It's not your fault. You have been wonderful to me."

"I can make some calls, find somewhere else for you to go."

"We'll find a place, Celine. We'll be all right," Audrey said, feeling strangely calm. Hadn't it been too much to hope that this moment would never come? Because deep inside, hadn't she known that it would?

AT NICHOLAS'S REQUEST, the taxi had followed the woman's small car out of Florence and onto the Autostrada, hanging far enough behind to stay out of sight.

She had taken the exit marked Certaldo and followed the next road for five or six miles. When she'd made a right-hand turn onto a smaller hard-top road, Nicholas had asked the driver to pull over and wait a minute. They followed the smaller road for a mile or so, taking a few right-hand turns. They came to a gravel driveway, dust still hanging in the air.

Nicholas asked the driver to let him out there. The man gave him a strange look but stated the fare. Nicholas paid him in Euros and got out. The taxi made a U-turn and left.

Huge old cypress trees lined either side of the road, throwing shadows across the sunlight. There was still time to let this go. He could be wrong again. Maybe he had imagined the woman's distress earlier. But something told him he hadn't. That same feeling pulled him forward, down the dusty road, his pace quickening with every stride.

AUDREY DIDN'T BOTHER with folding anything. She yanked their clothes from the drawers and dropped them in the suitcases.

Celine had gone back out to the shed to pack up her paints and brushes.

Sammy stood in the middle of the living room, his hand on George's head. "Why do we have to go, Mama?"

"I can't explain now, honey. We just have to hurry."

"But I don't want to leave."

Audrey stopped for a moment and looked at her son. "I'm sorry, baby." And she was. Sorry to have given him the kind of life she had dreamed of giving him, only to yank the entire thing up by the roots. But she had no choice. Would there ever be a time when she did have a choice?

Sammy turned away, his cheeks wet with solemn tears. He went to the living-room window, his back straight and tall as if he knew he had to be strong for her.

"Mama, there's a man standing outside in the yard."

Audrey dropped the suitcase. It made an awful clattering sound that reverberated through her like nails on glass. "Come away from the window, Sammy."

Sammy turned and ran to her side. "Who is it? Why are you so afraid?"

Footsteps sounded on the flagstone walkway and then a knock at the door. "Hello? I'm looking for someone. I'm hoping you can help me."

George barked.

Audrey went completely still. That voice. It couldn't be. She remembered Celine's description. *Good-looking. Tall, dark hair.* A wave of disbelief rolled over her, and she had to force herself to move. Still holding Sammy's hand, she crossed the living-room floor and opened the door.

NICHOLAS BLINKED and stepped back. "Audrey."

"My God," she said, her face white with shock. "Nicholas. What are you doing here?"

The words held anything but welcome. "I've been looking for you," he replied. *As if he could express why he had come.*

"Looking for me," she said.

The woman he had seen at the shop earlier walked into the room. She pointed a small gun at him, her mouth set with the resolve to use it.

Audrey glanced over shoulder. "It's okay, Celine. This is—"

"A friend," he said.

Celine looked at Audrey for confirmation. Audrey nodded. "Do you think you could take

Sammy to your house for a little while?" she asked.

"Of course." Celine gave Nicholas another assessing look, then took Sammy's hand and said, "Are you sure, Audrey?"

"Yes, it's okay."

Celine and Sammy left through the back door, the yellow Lab following behind them.

"May I come in?" Nicholas asked.

She nodded. He stepped inside and closed the door. One glance at the small living room made it clear that she had been leaving.

"I'm sorry for scaring you," he said. "I never intended that."

She swung around then, color slashed across each cheekbone. "Do you have any idea what you just did?"

"Audrey, I'm sorry—"

"You're sorry!" She came at him then, her hands balled into fists, pummeling at his chest. The blows stopped as suddenly as they had started, and great, heaving sobs shook through her.

"Audrey. I never meant to put you through that. You have to believe me."

Her weeping nearly tore him in half. It was as if years of sorrow had burst forth from her, a dam flooding land for the first time. Nicholas thought he could drown in the sound of it.

She looked up at him, her cheeks wet with tears. And he saw the shadow of horror as it flitted across her face, her disbelief at what she had done. "Oh, God," she said. She placed her palms on his chest, spreading her fingers wide as if she could take back what had happened.

Nicholas wrapped his arms around her then and held her there, not knowing what else to do.

CHAPTER THIRTEEN

AUDREY HAD no idea how long they stood that way. She only knew that she had been fooling herself to think she had felt safe before. Here, she felt safe. Here in the arms of a man who, for some reason, had gone to great lengths to find her. Who looked at her with something in his eyes she had never seen before, but that she felt deep within herself.

She pulled back, staring up at him, needing suddenly to see if she had imagined that look. It was still there, and it lit her up inside. He leaned in then and kissed her. A gentle touch that said more than any words possibly could.

She opened her mouth to his and returned his kiss, her arms slipping around his neck, a small sigh of longing melting into the kiss.

His hands were at her waist, one thumb stroking the skin beneath her sweater.

"Audrey." Her name on his lips said so many things. She heard them all. And yielded. He dipped his head and kissed her chin, the line of her jaw, her ear, his tongue flicking inside. Sensation skidded through her.

He stepped back, shoving his hands in his pockets as if otherwise he wouldn't be able to keep them off her. It was not an easy thing for Audrey to believe. She had long ago lost any vision of herself as attractive.

She turned away from him, went to the window and folded her arms across her chest, her body stiff and straight. "Why are you here?"

"I'm not sure I have an easy answer for that question."

She glanced over at him then. "Is this a game to you? Some whim you couldn't resist following?"

"No." He shook his head. "Audrey, no."

"What, then?"

"Jonathan came to see me after he discovered you were gone."

Audrey's heart thudded. "He didn't—"

"I've seen that kind of rage," he said. "And I've seen the result of it. I wanted to find you before he did."

"So you found me. That means he will, too."

He was quiet for a moment, as if he wanted to deny it. "I don't think he'll give up until he does."

"So what is your conclusion? That I should give up and go back? Accept that there is no place I can go where he can't—"

"Audrey."

His tone stole the rest of her response.

"I don't have any conclusions," he said. "I just needed to see for myself that you were all right."

The ticking of the clock by the door grew louder in the silence, the bald honesty in the admission undeniable. She let the words hang, not having the least idea what to do with them.

He came over to where she stood. "I know this must sound crazy, but from the moment I met you, there was this click inside me, like something I had expected for a long time finally happened. From that moment, it was like I didn't have a choice, Audrey, no matter how many times I told myself a smarter man would walk away and not look back."

"You should have," she said, but even to her own ears, the words did not sound convincing.

He reached out and touched her hair with the back of his fingers. "If you want me to leave, I will."

She felt as if she stood now at one end of a bridge, and once she crossed it, there would be no turning back.

But for the first time in a long, long while, Audrey wanted something for herself.

SHE CALLED Celine and asked if she could borrow her car to drive him back into Florence. Audrey felt her friend's curiosity through the line. "Can we talk about this later?" she asked.

"Of course," Celine said, worry etched on her forehead. "Just one question. Is he putting you at risk?"

"I don't think so."

"Just don't forget what you've been through to get this far."

"I know," Audrey said.

"Having said that, a man would have to go to an awful lot of trouble to track down a woman who didn't want to be found. That must mean something."

But Audrey didn't know what it meant. Only that she felt an unrelenting need to find out. "I'm not sure how long I'll be gone."

"Take your time. And don't worry about Sammy. He'll be fine with George and me."

"Thank you, Celine," she said, and inadequate as the words sounded, they were heartfelt.

AUDREY DROVE.

Nicholas sat in the passenger seat, a look of determined indifference on his face.

She glanced at him and felt a smile overcome her, a lightness in such utter contrast to her normal self that she hardly recognized it. "I thought you liked fast cars."

A Mercedes blew by them in the left lane, the air blast whooshing into Celine's small car like a bully throwing an elbow jab.

"Maybe this one's a little out of its league?"

"Would you like me to slow down?"

"Do I get points deducted if I say yes?"

"Not this time," she said.

Once they were in the city, Nicholas directed her down a few narrow streets to the Savoy Hotel where he was staying. They pulled up in front. Audrey left the engine running.

"Any way I can talk you into going to dinner with me?" he asked.

She was silent for a few moments, and then said, "You just did."

AUDREY WAITED in the small sitting area adjoining Nicholas's room while he showered. A pair of well-worn running shoes sat by a leather chair. A hardcover novel lay on the round table next to it. She stepped over to glance at the jacket. Faulkner.

She moved to the window, looking down on the street outside the hotel where Florentines lingered outside shop doors, chatting. It was nearly twilight, the sun slipping slowly beneath the city's horizon. Nicholas had left the door connecting the two rooms ajar, and she could hear the shower, a sudden thud as if he'd dropped the soap. There was an intimacy to being here in his hotel room that made Audrey realize just how far along this road she had come. She could not see what lay ahead, nor could she deny her desire to find out.

The water stopped. A door opened. She pictured him reaching for a towel, and imagined the bareness of his wide shoulders, the muscles in his long legs.

She closed her eyes, hoping to obliterate the image, but it was still there, along with a low burn of attraction that, if she were honest with herself, had started on New Year's Eve, the night they'd met. She felt, somehow, as if from that moment, she'd had no choice. Just as Nicholas had said. No choice.

It was crazy. Beyond crazy. And yet here she was in his hotel room, the last place in the world she would have pictured herself when she'd gotten up this morning. Undeniable, too, that it was where she wanted to be.

"Sorry to keep you waiting."

She turned from the window. He wore khaki pants and a blue-jean shirt with a white T-shirt showing at the neck. His hair was still damp, and he hadn't taken the time to shave, the dark stubble on his face adding to his appeal. "Your view is wonderful."

"A great place to people-watch."

"The pace of life is different here, isn't it?"

He came to the window and stood beside her so that their shoulders touched. Below, people wandered in and out of shop doors. Laughter tinkled up, caught in lovely echoes between the old buildings.

"I envy that," he said. "Sometimes I think we go at everything as if the clock is ticking. Days and whole months go by in a blur, and we can't possibly see the details of anything."

She was quiet for a moment, and then said, "Maybe people get so focused on being something that they forget to just be."

He turned to her, his eyes serious. "Do you think we could do that for a while, Audrey? Just be, and see where it takes us?"

It was a wonderful thought. And for once, Audrey didn't let herself dwell on the impossibilities of it. Their time here felt cut out from the rest of their lives, as if it had no before and would likely have no after. Only now.

THEY LEFT THE HOTEL and simply wandered, turning in whichever direction suited them, passing the Mercato Nuovo, a sixteenth-century straw market at the corner of Via Porta Rossa and Via Por Santa Maria where the vendors had packed up their leather goods for the day. They admired the wild boar fountain at the south end of the market, threw some coins in for luck and then walked on.

Night had fallen, and the streets were bathed in soft light. At some point, Nicholas reached for her hand, entwining his fingers with hers. And his touch felt good and right.

Most of the restaurants had menus posted on wooden stands outside their doors.

"Say when something looks good," Nicholas said.

"How about this one?"

They stopped at a small trattoria to glance at its daily menu. The smells wafting from inside were sales pitch enough.

The interior was low-lit with wall sconces, a vaulted ceiling and fresco walls. Round tables were covered in white tablecloths. A gray-haired woman with a kind smile appeared and welcomed them in Italian before directing them to a table tucked into a corner near the front window.

Nicholas held Audrey's chair and then sat down across from her. The woman handed them a set of menus which they studied for a few minutes. He ordered a bottle of wine. A young man brought it out right away, popped the cork, poured some into Nicholas's glass, then waited for his approval.

"Very good," Nicholas said.

The waiter smiled, then filled Audrey's glass before topping Nicholas's.

Once he'd gone, Nicholas clinked the edge of

his glass against hers. "To you, Audrey. A very brave woman."

The words caught her off guard, locking her throat so that her wine barely went down. "I'm not sure courage had anything to do with it."

"It has everything to do with it," he said gently.

She dropped her gaze, having long ago grown used to being torn down, to hearing her inadequacies cited again and again.

Nicholas asked about Sammy then, what he thought of Italy. Audrey began to talk, telling him how crazy Sammy was about George, about Celine and what a wonderful cook she was, about how she'd helped Audrey market her pots.

It was wonderful to be able to talk about her son. And Nicholas listened. Really listened. As if he found it all fascinating. As if he found her fascinating. No one had ever looked at her quite like this, as if she were the most interesting person in the room. Like the wine, the feeling was intoxicating.

The waiter returned with a salad of baby greens dressed in olive oil and sprinkled with grated Asiago cheese. They ate in silence for a few minutes, and even that was comfortable, as though they had done it before, and had no need to fill the quiet with meaningless chatter.

He added more wine to her glass and then his own.

The waiter brought their pasta, bowls of steaming fusilli in a cream sauce with baby peas and prosciutto. Every bite was simple and delicious.

They talked like two people who wanted to know everything there was to know about each other. He ended a sentence, and she started another where he left off, their words stitching together the pieces of their lives like thread in a patchwork quilt. She told him about her mother and father, her two brothers, both of whom were married with children.

"Did you see them often?" Nicholas asked.

Audrey shook her head. "No."

Quiet anger clouded his eyes. "He kept you from your family."

"I realize now that I let him," she said.

Nicholas changed the subject then. She could feel that he wanted to say more, but he didn't. He talked about his job as a prosecutor, and this was where his voice came to life.

"You loved your work there," Audrey said. "Why did you leave?"

He held up his glass and swirled the wine around the bowl once. "It just began to feel like the good never had a chance over the bad. Like being caught out in the middle of a blizzard with only a single shovel. You dig and dig, and it seems like you're making headway, but then the snow keeps coming, piling up around you, until it's over your shoulders. You can't move your arms, can't breathe anymore. You finally give up and just let it bury you."

Audrey couldn't pull her gaze from his face. She could see in his eyes a man who had once believed he would make a difference. "You must have been very good at what you did."

He lifted a shoulder. "I thought so for a long time."

"It must be a different world for you, working with Ross."

Nicholas poured them each more wine, then set the bottle down. "I resigned from Webster & Associates. I don't work for him anymore."

Audrey put down her fork and stared at him for a moment. "Why?"

"Let's just say we didn't see eye to eye on some of the things Ross chose to overlook."

"Me, you mean."

"For one. I won't deny that."

Audrey's heart responded to the seriousness in his voice. Suddenly, the walls of the tiny restaurant felt as if they were closing in around her. She stood, sliding back her chair. "I'll wait outside," she said and left.

NICHOLAS DROPPED some cash on the table and went after her.

He found her leaning against a lamppost, her

face pale, her hands clasped together in front of her. Nicholas felt a sharp stab of remorse for the turn their night had taken. He wished for some way to erase Jonathan's presence between them. Halfway around the world, it was as if he were here.

"What did you hope to prove in coming here, Nicholas?"

He stared at her for a long moment, and then said, "That I hadn't dreamed you. That you were real."

THEY WALKED BACK to the hotel, hands by their respective sides.

Outside the front door, she asked the valet to get her car and reached in her purse for the stub she had given him earlier. Nicholas felt the shift between them, a resignation on her part that had not been there before.

She looked up at him, one hand clutched tightly to the strap of her purse. "Thank you for the dinner. It was wonderful."

He studied her for a moment before asking, "Why do I have the feeling this is goodbye?"

"It can't be anything else."

"You're going to leave, aren't you?"

"I'll find somewhere. Please don't follow me this time, Nicholas."

"Will you spend the rest of your life running?"

he asked, jerking his fingers through his hair. "Is that how you want to live?"

The answer flitted across her face in the millisecond before she caught it and covered it up with acceptance. "You can't change this situation, Nicholas. I know that you want to, that some part of you needs to do so to set something right inside you. I don't know what that is, but whatever blame you've leveled at yourself, I can't be what changes it."

The valet pulled up with the car, got out and stood waiting by the open door.

Nicholas looked down at her, reaching for words but finding none.

She put her hand on his arm. "Thank you for caring about me. I won't forget that."

She stepped back, handed the valet some money, then got in the little car and drove off into the night.

AUDREY WENT straight to Celine's house to pick up Sammy. It was almost midnight when Celine opened the door. Audrey could see she had not slept. "I know," she said. "It's crazy."

Celine sighed and ran a hand through already tousled hair. "I don't have to tell you what the risks are."

"No."

"Just be careful," Celine said, reaching for Audrey's hand and giving it a squeeze, the concern in her eyes saying as much as any words could have. "You have so much to lose."

Audrey nodded once, not trusting her voice. All the way back from Florence, she had tried to lay out another plan for Sammy and her. The burden of it felt enormous, and she thought if she could sleep first, then she might be able to face the task.

They went to Celine's spare room where Sammy was curled up in the twin bed with George next to him. George opened his eyes, but did not raise his head.

"He can stay the night, Audrey," Celine said.

Seeing her son tucked in beside the dog he had come to love and would soon have to leave, Audrey did not have the heart to wake him. She hated to uproot him again, after he was just starting to settle in. She went over and kissed the top of his head, then came back out into the hallway. "Thank you, Celine."

"No thanks needed," she said. "I'll see you in the morning."

AUDREY SLEPT without dreaming.

A sound pulled her awake. She sat up, startled to see the room filled with light. She glanced at the clock. Eight already.

A knock sounded at the front door.

She swung out of bed and ran to the living-room window. A car sat in the little courtyard beside Celine's. Nicholas stood on the steps, hands in the pockets of his leather jacket.

Audrey opened the door, running a hand over her hair and tucking a few strands behind her ears.

He said nothing for a moment, his gaze dropping over her cotton pajamas down to her bare feet before following the same path back to her face. "I know it's early," he said, "but I was afraid you might leave before I got here."

She stared at him for a moment, not sure what to say. "You shouldn't have come."

"Spend the day with me, Audrey. That's all I'll ask. Just the day. Whatever decision you make then, I'll accept."

She should say no, end this here before it flared into something more out of control than it already was. But she felt the weakness within herself; it slipped through her veins like warm brandy, altering reality, if only temporarily.

She wanted the day with him. Could one day really change anything?

CHAPTER FOURTEEN

ONCE AUDREY HAD DRESSED, she made coffee, and they both drank a cup on the small terrace at the rear of the house. The silence between them was peaceful, expectant, as if their time together held magic in its unfolding. When Audrey said she needed to get Sammy, Nicholas offered to walk with her. And that was how the day began. Nothing planned or discussed. It was as if he had been here all along, slipping into their lives with an unobtrusiveness that felt entirely too right.

At Celine's house, Audrey introduced Nicholas to Sammy as a friend. She could see the immediate wall of reserve in her son's eyes. He walked down the hill to their home with his hand inside hers. Nicholas didn't try to win him with small talk. He walked a few spaces apart from them, and once they were back at the house, he stayed out in the yard, tossing a ball in the air.

Sammy stood at the living-room window watching him. "Did Daddy send him here, Mama?"

Audrey came out of the kitchen where she had just started to make a pot of homemade soup. She crossed the floor and put a hand on her son's shoulder. "No, baby. Nicholas is someone I met before we left. He's a nice man."

Sammy weighed the words. "How do you know?"

Audrey sighed, then dropped to her knees, one hand on each of his arms. "One of the hardest things for me right now is trust. Believing other people are going to be different. I know it's the same for you. Maybe we can both work on that together. What do you think?"

Sammy looked down, then met her eyes. "What if he turns out not to be nice?"

"I think the biggest mistake either of us could make would be to judge the rest of the world by your father's actions. Because if we do, we're going to miss out on a lot of good things."

Hearing herself say the words, Audrey recognized the truth in them. It would be so easy to let the past shape the rest of her life. With sudden certainty, she knew she wanted something different.

Sammy glanced out the window to where Nicholas was still tossing the ball in the air.

"Do you think he might want to play catch with me?"

Tears blurred her vision. "I bet he would," she said.

THEY'D BEEN THROWING the ball back and forth for an hour or more, neither of them saying a word. Nicholas felt as if Sammy's trust were too tenuous for him to do anything more than stand on the other end of the yard, pitching and catching.

He could see the stiffness in the boy, the lack of confidence in the way he threw. He reminded Nicholas of Lola when he'd first brought her home, the way she looked as though she were walking on glass, afraid the ground might shatter beneath her feet.

And so, he just threw the ball. Back and forth. Over and over. After one particularly good throw from Sammy, he said, "Hey, you've been holding out on me!"

Sammy glanced up, surprise in his eyes. A shy smile touched his lips.

"That was a great one."

The smile grew. "Do you have a son?"

"No. But if I ever do, I hope he can throw like that."

They threw in silence again for a while, and then Sammy said, "You're not going to tell my dad we're here, are you?"

The words took a chink out of Nicholas's heart. He dropped the ball to his side, crossed the yard and knelt in front of the boy. "No," he said. "I'm not."

Sammy looked away, then turned back. "Good," he said. "My mom is happy here."

"I know. And I'm glad."

The boy nodded once, the worry in his eyes giving way to gratitude. "Thank you," he said.

AUDREY WATCHED from the window, wondering what they were saying to each other. Nicholas put his hand on Sammy's shoulder, squeezed, then turned to walk across the yard.

They started throwing again, and she could almost see her son's defensive barriers crumble. He had been hurt so many times by his father's refusal to do the things with him that other fathers did with their sons. She had tried so hard to make up for it, but she could not take away the sting of rejection.

Without question, Nicholas's presence here put her at risk. But somehow, she could not bring herself to regret that he had found them.

THEY SPENT the rest of the day doing ordinary stuff. It was the best day Nicholas could remember in a long time. They ate lunch in the shaded backyard. Audrey's soup with a loaf of Celine's homemade bread. She found a bottle of wine in the pantry, and they sipped from their glasses while Sammy played on the tree swing at the edge of the yard.

"I can see why you love it here," Nicholas said.

Audrey nodded. "It's so peaceful."

"Sammy's a really special boy."

She glanced up at Nicholas. "He is. And his father never saw that."

Nicholas frowned. "He obviously knows you love him."

Audrey ran a thumb around the rim of her glass. "He was a happy, sunny baby. He almost never cried. When he was old enough to become aware of things, I could see it changing him."

"I don't see it in him now," Nicholas said, his gaze on the boy.

"He's better. Just in the time we've been here. It's amazing."

He was quiet for a moment, and then asked, "Did you ever try to leave before?"

Audrey's eyes took on a faraway look, and Nicholas wished he hadn't said anything.

"Yes," she admitted. "Three times. The last time I just put Sammy in the car and started driving. No idea where I was going. Just away. Some place where he could never find us. We got as far as Virginia when Sammy got sick. I took him to a doctor who thought it was probably a virus, and that he would be fine in twenty-four hours. We stayed in a hotel room for two days. I kept taking his temperature, agonizing every time it went up instead of down. He kept getting worse, and I finally had to take him to the emergency room. I just wanted him to be all right. When they asked for my insurance information, I didn't want to give it to them. But they said we would have to go across town to another hospital if I didn't have it. I couldn't risk delaying Sammy's treatment. Anyway, that's how he found us the last time."

Nicholas listened with a heavy feeling in his stomach, imagining what it must have felt like to wait there, knowing that Jonathan was coming. His fists tightened with the urge to hurt the other man as he had hurt Audrey.

"Hey, Mama, look!"

Sammy had climbed up in the tree and was hanging by skinny arms from one of the lower branches.

"Be careful, honey," Audrey called out.

Nicholas reached over and took her hand in his. "You're going to be all right this time," he said. "Both of you."

She looked at him, wiped the back of her other hand across her eyes, nodded and smiled. "Yeah," she said. "I think we are."

NICHOLAS DROVE back to Florence after dinner that night, claiming he didn't want to wear out his welcome. Before leaving, he'd asked if he could come back the following day. She'd been unable to say no, watching him drive off down the gravel road with an undeniable sense of regret. She would have to move on. She knew this, but she couldn't bring herself to do so just yet.

"He *is* nice, Mama."

Audrey turned from the window. Sammy stood just outside the kitchen, a hopeful look on his face. She crossed the floor and dropped to her knees, wrapping her arms around him. "I'm sorry that our life was so hard before, honey. I wish—"

Sammy pulled back, the look in his eyes far beyond his years. "I don't want to think about that anymore. I like our life now. Let's just think about that part."

She kissed his forehead, her heart aching with love for him. "Deal," she said.

THE FOLLOWING MORNING, Nicholas pulled into the driveway in a red BMW convertible he had traded his other rental in for.

"Wow," Sammy declared, bolting out the door at the sight of him. "Can we go for a ride?"

Nicholas grinned, looking up at Audrey where she stood at the front step. "I was hoping I could take you and your mom to lunch."

"Sounds fun," she said, smiling.

They took their time on the winding roads leading to the small hill town of Certaldo Alto. They parked and walked up the cobblestone streets, ducking into a few shops. The town was mostly residential, few tourists in sight. The smells of home-cooking, bread in ovens and the delicious fragrance of herbs drifted through open windows. They circled the entire town, then decided to walk back to where they had spotted a small restaurant that opened at noon.

The hostess spoke no English, but they were able to communicate well enough to ask for a table. She seated them on an enclosed porch with casement windows thrown open to one of the most beautiful views Audrey had ever seen. Stucco houses with clay-tile roofs dotted the landscape as far as they could see. Olive trees and grapevines lined the rolling hillsides.

"It's incredible," she said, once the hostess had left them with menus. "You can see for miles. What a perfect place."

Nicholas nodded, his gaze locking with hers. "Perfect," he said.

It was clear that he meant more than the view. Warmth flooded her cheeks, and she looked away, somehow amazed that a man like the one sitting across from her might truly be attracted to her.

They started their meal with a delicious trio of pastas, all of which they sampled. The bread was wonderful, freshly made that morning, according to the waiter who spoke a little English.

Another couple arrived with a son close to Sammy's age. He approached their table with a shy smile, waving a Game Boy at Sammy and saying something in Italian.

"Mama, can I play?" Sammy asked.

"Sure," Audrey said, "just stay in sight, okay?"

The two boys found a bench at the other end of the porch and began playing.

Nicholas smiled. "Universal, huh?"

"Apparently," Audrey said.

He leaned forward to rest his forearms on the table. "Thank you for coming with me today."

"Thank you for asking. It's incredible."

"Someone at the hotel recommended it. A place you won't forget, he said."

The waiter arrived, and Nicholas ordered a bottle of wine which appeared at their table in no time. The waiter filled their glasses, placed another basket of still steaming bread in front of them, then made some recommendations for their lunch. Audrey ordered for Sammy and her. Once Nicholas had chosen, the waiter left them alone.

"Yesterday, when you were talking about your work," Audrey said, "it sounded as if it was something you'd been called to do."

He looked out at the incredible view before

them, then met her gaze. "I guess maybe it was."
He hesitated for a long moment, and then continued, "I had a sister." His expression was blank but
for a flicker of something old and painful in his
eyes. "At fifteen she was raped and murdered."

Shock rolled over Audrey in a wave. She saw
the pain in his face and regretted forcing him into
the revelation. "Oh, Nicholas. I'm so sorry. I
didn't mean to—"

"It's okay," he said.

"I'm sorry," she said again, not knowing what
else to say.

He was quiet for a few moments. "It was my
fault. I was supposed to pick her up after a football game. I had a girlfriend, and I let myself get
distracted. By the time I realized what time it
was—" His voice broke.

Audrey reached across, took his hand and
pressed it between both of hers.

They sat that way for a long time. "What about
your parents?" she asked finally, her voice raspy
with disbelief.

"They live in Augusta."

"And you don't see them?"

He lifted a shoulder, the pain in his eyes deep-
ening. "I guess I don't think they should have to
be reminded."

Audrey sat back in her seat, her gaze still on

him. "So they lost two children that day, not just one?"

Nicholas glanced away, and then said, "I guess they did."

With this glimpse into his past, Audrey understood so much more about this man who had gone to such lengths to find her. He had known pain in his life as well, and she knew suddenly that it had influenced the choices he made and most likely still did.

In this, they were the same.

THE SOMBERNESS of that conversation tempered the remainder of the day with a kind of quiet reflection. Audrey somehow felt closer to Nicholas, as if he had shown her something of himself he did not often reveal.

After lunch, they walked through the idyllic little town. Sammy raced ahead and then darted back to report in on some marvelous sight he had just spotted.

For Audrey, it was almost scary, this connection. Not just between Nicholas and her, but between the three of them. Nicholas spoke to Sammy with respect and interest, and she could already see the effect of that on her son.

They returned to the house early that evening. Celine had left a tureen of stew and a loaf of bread just inside the door, and Audrey invited Nicholas to stay and eat with them.

"I should head back," he said, surprising her.

"Oh," she said, admittedly a little disappointed. "I—well, it was a wonderful day. Thank you."

"Could we do it again tomorrow? I was also told San Gimignano is a must see."

"I can't tomorrow," Sammy piped in. "You said I could go with Celine to George's agility class. I really want to go."

"I forgot," Audrey said, running a hand across his hair. "What time is the class?"

"One o'clock," Sammy said.

"We could wait until they get back," Nicholas suggested.

"The last time it was after dinner," Sammy said.

Audrey looked at Nicholas. "Maybe we could go and be back by then."

"That sounds good," he said.

"Okay."

"Okay." He stared at her for a moment, the heat of something she was afraid to identify in his eyes. He stepped back then, quickly, as if he didn't trust himself to stay.

Later that evening, Audrey made herself a cup of decaffeinated coffee with the French press she had borrowed from Celine, then sat outside drinking it and going over the day as the moon threw light across her small yard. She thought about Nicholas's sister and how that tragedy had shaped the man he was. And of how it answered so many of her questions about him and allowed her to see him from a very different perspective. With this new insight, the tiny crack in her heart where her feelings for him had already wedged themselves now widened and became a chasm through which any remaining resistance washed away in a great rushing current.

THE NEXT DAY dawned sunny and warm, the sky a perfect cloudless blue. Celine and George picked Sammy up just after eleven. "Why don't you just let him spend the night with me?" Celine asked. "Then you won't have to worry about what time to be back."

"You've been too good to me, Celine," Audrey said.

"I love having him stay. It's a treat for me. Not to mention for George."

"Are you sure?"

"Positive. And Audrey?"

"Yeah?"

"You're not doing your son any favors by walking around with that noose of guilt around your neck. Go and enjoy the day. You deserve it."

She showered, washed and dried her hair, slipped on a sleeveless white dress with a scooped neck and a loose flowing skirt. She took extra time with her makeup and felt like a teenager getting ready for a first date.

Nicholas arrived a short while later, the look on his face when she opened the door justifying all of her efforts.

"Hi," she said.

"Hi." A smile touched his mouth. "You look incredible."

She dropped her eyes, not used to such honest appreciation. "Thanks. If you're ready, we can—"

"—go," he finished. "I'm ready. I've actually been ready since four this morning, but I thought if I came that early it might come across as overly anxious."

She looked at him then and laughed, relaxing. They drove with the top down. Audrey tipped her head against the seat and let the sun warm her face. They rode for ten or fifteen minutes, silent, but at ease with one another. Nicholas glanced away from the wheel, his gaze searching out hers. "Sure you're all right leaving Sammy?"

"Celine is wonderful with him. And George is the dog he always wanted."

"How did you meet Celine?"

"I hadn't, actually, until I got here." She hesitated, remembering the day she'd arrived, how welcome the sight of that small house had been. "The address was given to me by an underground network that helps women…like me."

He was quiet for a moment, and then said, "How did you find out about it?"

"A nurse I met in the emergency room," she replied, the words somehow not so difficult to say anymore. "She had been where I was. Recognized the signs, I guess."

"And?" he asked, his voice soft.

"I e-mailed the contact person for the organization. Told her I wanted to leave the country. And she sent me here, to Celine."

"She's a nice woman."

"Yes, she is." Audrey studied his handsome profile, his set jaw. She wondered at the thoughts going through his mind.

He suddenly turned the car into the parking lot of a small restaurant and stopped at one end where there were no other vehicles. "I have something to give you," he said.

Audrey stared at him, unsettled by the change in his voice.

He reached inside his jacket, pulled out a manila envelope and handed it to her.

"What is it?" she asked.

"Information," he said. "In case you ever need it."

Her stomach dropped. Without asking, she knew this was about Jonathan. "Nicholas—"

"Please," he said. "I hope that you never will. But if you do, I want you to use it."

She had always wondered about her husband's business practices and suspected that Ross's willingness to accommodate Jonathan extended to his construction company as well. "And how did you come across this?"

"That's not important."

She studied him for a moment. "It is," she said. "This isn't you. You compromised your ethics."

He held her gaze, and then said, "As much as I might wish it were different, the world doesn't always operate to suit my ethics. That's a lesson I've had repeated enough times to know it's true."

He took the envelope from her, folded it in half, then tucked it inside her purse. "I don't want this day to be about that," he said. "I very much want it to be about us."

She glanced at her purse, then back at him and nodded once. "So do I," she said.

THEY GOT BACK on the road and drove for a good while, staying away from the autostrada, following curving roads that wound through small town after small town. They passed farmhouses and fields of dark, rich dirt, newly plowed for planting. They passed groves of olive trees and small, family vineyards seamed into nearly vertical hillsides.

They came to a small sign that read San Gimignano and turned there.

A hill town overlooking the Elsa Valley, San Gimignano was established in the tenth century. Audrey passed along Celine's explanation of how the town prospered with the wealthiest families building towers that dominated the landscape.

Nicholas parked the car just outside the town walls, and they walked in.

"It feels like stepping into another time," he said.

They started at the foot of the main street and wandered store to store. There were bakeries with fresh-out-of-the-oven rolls and loaves of bread. Stores with fine leather goods. A small gallery that displayed the works of local artists.

Halfway up the hill, they stopped outside a small restaurant where the most incredible smells permeated the air. Tomato sauce, garlic and basil.

"Are you hungry?" Nicholas asked.

"Starving," she confessed.

"Then let's eat," he said, taking her hand and leading her inside.

They sated themselves with the local specialty, linguine in a saffron sauce. Ate bread dipped in rich olive oil, and drank red wine made from the restaurant owner's vineyard, the woman smiling with pleasure to see that they liked it.

They talked about everything, little stuff, big stuff. And again, it felt strange to be sitting across from a man who was interested in her opinions, who wanted to hear what she had to say.

She took a sip of her wine. "Sometimes," she said, "I can't believe life can be like this."

"Like what?" he asked softly.

"Not having to constantly monitor what I say or do."

"Was it always like that between you?"

"Not in the beginning, no. He was kind to me. In a different way than I was used to…"

"When did things change?"

"We'd been married a year the first time he…hit me," she said, flinching at the sound of the words.

Nicholas reached out and put his hand over hers.

Something in his touch gave her the courage to go on, to say what she'd never said to anyone else before. "At first, I thought it had to be a mistake…an accident. How could he mean to do that? Or maybe I'd done something to cause it. I tried so hard to figure out what it was, to make sure I never did it again."

"It didn't matter though, did it?" he asked, his voice threaded with quiet anguish.

She shook her head, her hands clasped around

her glass. "No. For so long, I kept thinking it would get better, that somehow I could make it work. But it was the opposite. It seemed like the more I tried, the worse things became."

"Audrey. I'm sorry."

She bit her lip, looked down, then met his gaze. "I think back and remember things that happened in the beginning, things that should have made me wonder…I ask myself why I didn't see…or why I wouldn't let myself. But then the answers don't really matter. I look at Sammy, and I can't regret any of the choices I've made."

Nicholas was silent for a moment, and then said, "The thing you have to know is that none of this was your fault, Audrey. None of it. You have to let yourself believe that."

She nodded once. "I'm working on it."

They left the restaurant a little while later, both of them quiet under the weight of everything that had been said. They continued up the winding cobblestone streets to the towers at the top of the town. Each tower had once represented the wealth of the family who had built it. In the thirteenth century, there had been seventy-two towers. There were only fourteen left now, the others having fallen into disrepair when San Gimignano went through a decline in prosperity.

Nicholas and Audrey climbed one of the middle towers, the tallest remaining. At the top, Audrey went to one of the small windows that looked out over the countryside beyond the town. Nicholas stood behind her.

She shook her head, amazed. "It's incredible, isn't it?"

"Yes," he said. "Incredible."

She felt his gaze on her, something in his voice telling her he was going to touch her. She closed her eyes, hoping she wasn't wrong. Here in this town that felt cut away from everything, Audrey felt as if they, too, had been given this piece of time for themselves. And she wanted it as she had wanted few things in her life.

Need sparked low inside her. She had not asked for it, had not been looking for it, but this connection she felt to Nicholas was like finding something infinitely precious. She wanted to hold onto it even though she knew it was impossible.

His hands dropped to her shoulders, a question in his touch. She answered by leaning back into his solid chest. His hands slid under her arms, his palms flattening against her belly.

She turned and looked up and let him see what she felt. She trusted him—and knew somehow that her fear of trusting again would never be put to test by this man.

"Audrey." He kissed her then, his arms tightening around her waist, lifting her up and into him so that her feet left the floor.

He spun them around and leaned his back against the stone wall behind them, pulling her as close as it was possible for two fully dressed people to get.

She felt dizzy with longing. He took in her face, as if memorizing every angle, dimple, freckle. No one had ever looked at her this way, made her feel desirable without guilt or manipulation.

And then with a jumble of emotion in her heart, she kissed him, urgent and needful, wanting to give even as she took.

Outside, birds trilled. The sun dipped into the open archway, throwing light onto their faces, leaving the rest of them in shadow. They kissed for a long time, as if nothing else mattered now or ever would.

Finally, Nicholas pulled back, ran a thumb across the line of her jaw, then against her lips where his mouth had just been. "Let's find a place," he said.

And for Audrey, there was only one answer.

CHAPTER FIFTEEN

HIGH UP at the top of the town was a small hotel with a heavy wood door and a plaque with a five-star inscription. They arrived there breathless, climbing the main street with the kind of intent that blanks out everything else but the need to be alone.

At least this was what Audrey felt, what she sensed in Nicholas's long purposeful strides. There was a rightness to what she felt that did not need explanation or justification. It seemed simple, this urgency, and as basic as breathing, basic and yet without it, life could not go on.

Audrey waited by the enormous door while Nicholas went to the front desk and requested a room. The transaction was mercifully quick. And since they had no luggage, the bellman nodded in understanding when Nicholas turned down his offer to show them the room. Instead, he pointed out the elevator, punched the button for the fourth floor and sent them on their way.

As soon as the doors closed, Nicholas turned to her. "Was that too awful?"

"No," she said.

He reached for her hand, wrapping it in his. And then the elevator stopped. The doors opened. He let her step out first, then followed, still holding her hand.

The room was at the end of the hall. With the key, Nicholas opened the door, then closed it behind her.

"It's beautiful," she said. Against one wall was an old dark wood bed covered with a heavy damask comforter and a half dozen oversize pillows. Audrey went to the window. Like the tower they'd climbed earlier, this view took in the Tuscan countryside beyond the walled city.

Nicholas came to the window and stood behind her. She closed her eyes for a moment, then turned to him, putting a hand on his chest. He looked down at her, as if again memorizing her face, then lifted her hand to his lips and kissed the palm.

The look in his eyes filled Audrey with a simultaneous twist of happiness and panic. She had nothing to offer him. No life of her own. No future painted out into which he might eventually blend.

And she was a woman who would always be looking over her shoulder, never able to trust that the present could be more than what it was.

Nicholas cupped her face with both hands.

"Don't do that," he said, seeing what she was unable to hide. "For now, this is enough."

Audrey blinked, letting the words sway her worried heart. She did not want to think beyond this moment, to what might or might not be. For now, she just wanted this. Wanted him.

They held each other with uncensored care and deliberation. His touch had the power to heal, to erase inch by inch the scars she had thought she would carry forever, certain that their depth would prevent her from ever feeling anything close to what she felt now.

He pulled back and looked down at her with a mix of admiration and desire in his eyes. "You are so incredibly beautiful," he said.

Audrey glanced away, not knowing what to do with the sincerity in his voice. She felt unworthy of it, and yet at the same time, felt his vulnerability, his desire to convince her he meant what he said. "How did this happen?" she asked.

"The two of us being here?"

She shook her head.

"What?" he urged softly.

She met his questioning gaze. "Someone like me meeting someone like you."

"Audrey." Her name sounded as if it had been ripped from his throat. "You have no idea what I see when I look at you, do you?"

She bit her lip. "I feel like I don't deserve what's in your eyes."

"I'll tell you what I see," he said. "A woman who makes me want to be what I once hoped to be."

She put her arms around his neck and held on, something giving way within her, as if she had been keeping back some piece of herself, afraid to make herself that vulnerable.

He scooped her up and carried her to the bed, lowering her somewhere near the middle and then lying down beside her. Audrey's head slipped between the two pillows. He pulled one off, and she laughed, putting her hand at the back of his neck and pulling him to her, kissing him with longing and need.

They took their time with it, the afternoon sun warm across the bed. He undressed her, removing her clothes with a kind of reverence that she thought it would take a long time to accept as real. He stood then and unbuttoned his shirt, his eyes never leaving hers.

The shadows in the room grew long. And if it wasn't love, it was the closest Audrey had ever known.

THE SUN HAD DROPPED low in the sky when Nicholas awoke with Audrey still curled in the curve of his arm. He brushed a kiss across her forehead.

He'd had women in his life. It was not something he could deny. But there had never been a woman like this one. Not for him. And without knowing the why of it, he knew there would never be another.

Before, he had not known she was what he was waiting for. But he knew it now. He could not explain his certainty—he simply knew it to be truth.

And having found her, he also knew he could not let her go.

He'd had only to look in Audrey's eyes a short while ago, before they'd made love, to see that she believed they had no future. Somehow, he had to make her see that they had a right to it, that her life was her own, that she could not continue to live in the shadow of Jonathan's threats.

Just the thought filled him with a rage so intense it felt as if it were burning a hole inside him. He had learned long ago that the world was stitched together with injustices. He'd spent his adult life trying to right as many of them as he could, only to realize that he was never going to make a difference.

He'd accepted that and tried to point his life in another direction and had discovered that he couldn't live with himself wearing those shoes. He couldn't turn his head. He couldn't walk away. Not from whatever small differences he might make in the work he had once loved. And not from this woman who had unknowingly forced him to turn the mirror back at himself and reminded him of who it was he had once wanted to be. He wanted to be that person again. For himself. And for her.

LATER, THEY LAY IN BED, her head on his shoulder, her palm on his chest. It was difficult to find the words, but she needed to say them. "There's never been anything like this for me."

He smoothed his hand across her hair. "I know we're talking about different things, Audrey, but I feel the same."

She raised up on one elbow, met his serious gaze with a questioning look.

"I've spent my life avoiding anything that felt remotely close to the real thing," he said. "Turns out I didn't know what it was, anyway. But I do now."

"And you're not running?"

"I'm not running."

Audrey splayed her fingers across the muscles of his abdomen. She held the words deep inside her, protecting them as she would a candle whose small, vulnerable flame she did not want to let burn out.

AROUND SIX O'CLOCK, Audrey called Celine to say they would be late. She got the machine and left a message with the number of the hotel in case Celine wanted to call back. She felt a little strange openly acknowledging what they were doing, but somehow she knew the other woman would be happy for her.

They ordered room service for dinner, taking their time with their food, enjoying it as they enjoyed each other. For Audrey, the hours were a gift in a life long devoid of such luxuries as tenderness.

It was nearly eleven by the time they arrived at Celine's. Audrey had called again before they left San Gimignano. Celine hadn't answered, but since she usually went to bed early, Audrey decided she was probably asleep and hadn't heard the phone.

The house was dark when Nicholas stopped the car in her driveway. "Celine must have forgotten to leave the outside light on," Audrey said, opening her door. "I'll just run in and get Sammy."

"I'll come with you," Nicholas said.

Halfway to the front door, Audrey heard a noise. "That sounds like George barking. From the backyard." She frowned. "Celine never leaves him out."

"Hold on," Nicholas said. "Let me grab a flashlight. There was one in the glove compartment."

Audrey started around the house, unsettled by the dog's barking which had picked up in intensity. Nicholas was right behind, arcing the light across the backyard. They followed the sound to the small potting shed at the far corner. The dog was whining now, scratching frantically at the door.

Nicholas pulled it open, and the dog lunged

out, running past them to the front of the house, barking furiously.

"Something is wrong," Audrey said, her heart in her throat.

Nicholas grabbed her hand, and they ran after George, now scratching at the door.

"Celine?" Audrey called out. "Celine, are you there?"

Nicholas turned the knob. It was locked.

"Let's try the side door," Audrey said, and they sprinted back around the house.

It, too, was locked.

"We'll have to break a window." He grabbed a rock from Celine's flower bed.

The urgency in George's panic-filled barking, struck Audrey with terror. Nicholas tapped the pane at the corner of the door. When it shattered, he reached in and unlocked it. It swung open, and George leaped past them, still barking.

"Celine? Sammy?" Audrey called out, hearing the panic in her own voice.

They followed George through the house. He had stopped at Celine's bedroom door, again whining frantically.

Nicholas opened the door, while dread ran through Audrey's veins. There was Celine on a chair in the middle of the room. Her hands were bound behind her, each foot tied to a leg of the chair. Her mouth had been covered with duct tape. Tears ran down her face and left wet splotches on her jeans.

Audrey did not have to ask because she already knew the answer.

Sammy was gone.

"A MAN," Celine said once Nicholas had eased the tape away from her mouth. "We were outside this afternoon, and he just walked into the backyard. I never heard a car. He locked George in the shed and forced me into the house. My God, Audrey, I'm so sorry," she said. "I'm so sorry."

Audrey sank down onto the bed, clasping her hands in her lap. "Did Sammy know the man?"

Celine shook her head. "No. He told Sammy his father had sent him."

Fear turned Audrey's skin cold. "Was Sammy all right?" she asked, barely able to get the words out.

"He's a brave boy, Audrey."

"We'll find him," Nicholas said, his voice ragged. "I promise."

"I have to go back," she said, feeling her new life collapse around her. The day had been too perfect. She should have known it could not end that way. Because if life had taught her anything in these past ten years, it was that happiness always came with a price.

IT WAS his fault.

The words played through Nicholas's head over and over, the same refrain he had heard all these years since his sister's death.

He'd led them right to Audrey. He'd thought he'd been so careful. That it was impossible anyone could have followed him.

They were in the car on the way to the airport. Nicholas had his passport. He didn't want to waste time going back to the hotel for things he could replace. Audrey had grabbed a few things from her house, telling him in a numb voice that Sammy's passport was gone but hers had been left. On instructions from Jonathan, no doubt. The son of a bitch had known that by taking Sammy he would force her to come back.

He had to make this right. Somehow, he had to make this right. He reached for her hand, holding it in his. But hers remained limp, as if there were no longer any feeling there at all.

THE AIRPLANE RACED down the runway and then lifted high into the sky. Sammy looked out the window at the disappearing ground below, his hands clenching the chair's armrests.

The man beside him leaned over, his voice close to Sammy's ear. "Remember, you just do what I tell you, and you'll be okay. If you don't, you'll never see that mama of yours again."

Sammy stared out the window at the clouds below the plane. His chest hurt with a sudden yearning for his mother and their new life. He never should have believed it would last. He'd wanted it to so badly.

All the while he'd known that nothing good ever did.

AUDREY AND NICHOLAS landed some twelve hours after they'd left Florence. They caught a connecting flight out of New York to Atlanta. Audrey had not slept, but had sat staring out the window, playing out a dozen different scenarios for what lay ahead.

But she always came back to the same one. Nothing had changed. Jonathan was never going to let her go. She'd been a fool to think she could actually escape him. And now he had Sammy. Just the thought tightened her throat, filled her with a choking need to put her hands on her son, to know that he was all right. Just when she felt herself sinking beneath the weight of her fear, she realized that it was her he wanted. Not Sammy. Sammy was nothing more than insurance to Jonathan. Above all else, she hated him for that.

In the seat beside her, Nicholas sat solemn-faced. She knew he blamed himself. She wished she could find the words to make him understand that in the end it wouldn't have mattered. The outcome would have been the same.

He couldn't help her. She'd told him that from the beginning. But he hadn't believed her, and the funny thing was, she'd actually begun to think she'd been wrong. She'd been right, though, and she knew now that this was something she would have to finish alone.

Nicholas had left his car at the airport. They took the shuttle to the long-term parking lot, and he pulled out into the merging traffic with a grim set to his mouth.

"Could we go by your house first?" she asked. "I think a shower would help me think more clearly."

He glanced at her, obviously surprised. "Are you sure?"

"Yes," she said. "I'm sure."

NICHOLAS LIVED in an older neighborhood in Buckhead. Audrey followed him inside his house and he led her to a guest bedroom with a connecting bath. "I won't be long," she said.

"Okay." He pulled the door closed, and she locked it behind her. She went into the bathroom and turned on the shower. A pang of guilt hit her for the deceit. But this was something she had to do herself. Face Jonathan alone without putting Nicholas or anyone else at risk.

She waited a couple of minutes, then opened the door and stepped out into the hall. From the next bedroom, she could hear another shower running.

Closing the door behind her, she ran down the stairs and out of the house.

THE SHOWER did him good, lifting the fog clouding his mind, muddled as it was with lack of sleep and the kind of anger that can lead a man to do things he will surely regret.

It would be easy to lose his head and take care of Jonathan Colby in the only language the man seemed to understand.

But then that would be putting himself on the same level, and that was the last thing he wanted. And the last thing Audrey needed.

He pulled on clean jeans and a sweatshirt, unable to shake the memory of the look in Jonathan's eyes when he'd said he'd find her. The man believed he had rights to her in some demented way that Nicholas would never understand.

Just the thought of what he might do to her left Nicholas cold. But he would be with her. He would make sure she was safe. He had to.

From the hall, he heard the shower still running.

He knocked on the door of the guest bedroom. "Audrey?"

No answer. He waited a minute, then knocked again, before stepping inside the room. "Are you all right?" he called out. "Audrey!"

When no answer came, he flung open the bathroom door. But the glass-enclosed shower was empty. She wasn't here. Panic cut off the air to his lungs.

She had gone without him.

THE TAXI pulled up in front of the house, its screeching brakes strumming Audrey's already strung-out nerves.

All the way here, she'd focused her thoughts on Sammy, praying that he would be here, that he was all right. She could think of nothing else.

She paid the driver and got out. She'd left her keys behind when she'd fled this house, thinking she would never be back or perhaps it had been nothing more than a symbol of what she'd hoped would be true. At the front door, she closed her eyes for a moment, sending up another silent prayer for Sammy's safety. Strange as it felt, she knocked.

The longest minute of her life passed. And then the door opened.

Jonathan stood with his arms folded across his

chest, looking down at her with a complacency that told her he was not surprised to see her. "Hello, Audrey," he said.

"Where is he?" she asked, trying to keep her voice steady.

He stared at her for a long moment, his eyes dark with the kind of anger she knew too well. "What kind of greeting is that? At least come in."

"Jonathan—"

"Come in, Audrey," he said, his voice smooth as glass.

She stepped inside, her heart pounding. He closed the door behind her with a menacing click that sent echoes of the past rippling through her. She turned and said, "I need to see him."

"He isn't here."

"What have you done with him?" The question was edged with hysteria. She'd held it back all these hours during the plane trip, but now it felt as if it were taking over inside her, and she could barely control the urge to slap the smugness from his face.

"Don't worry. He's somewhere safe."

"I want him back, Jonathan."

He smiled a smile that did not reach his eyes. "So now you know how it feels to have your son taken away. Your own family."

"You left me no choice," she said, shaking her head.

"Oh, you always had a choice." He reached behind him, pulled a knife from the back of his pants, slipped it out of its leather case and held it to the light, its sharp edge glinting. "Did you really think you'd get away with this, Audrey? Didn't I tell you what would happen if you left me again?"

Audrey backed away. "Jonathan—"

"You've made a fool of me. My own wife. How can I just let that pass?"

Audrey's eyes never left the knife. She forced herself to breathe evenly, willing the panic aside. "Put that away, Jonathan."

He laughed, a harsh, empty sound, and moved toward her, forcing her farther into the living room, the look on his face one of resolve. He lunged for her then, knocking her to the floor. She struggled to get up, but he pinned her with an elbow to her neck, cutting off her air.

"I gave you everything a woman could possibly want," he said in a deadly voice. "And you threw it back in my face. As if it were nothing."

Red-hot anger set her on fire. She pushed at his arm and turned her head, gasping for air. "All I ever wanted was a home where my son could feel safe. Where I didn't have to worry about the next time you would explode or what I would do to cause it."

He put one hand around her throat, squeezing. The other hand held the knife above her. "I told you I'd never let anyone else have you. Do you expect me to go back on my word?"

Audrey felt the rage in his gaze and knew that this scene had been inevitable.

"I should have tried to talk to you before I left," she said, turning the blame on herself in one last hope of calming him.

He went still, his expression icy. He placed the blade against her throat. "Before you started screwing Wakefield, you mean?"

Tears welled in her eyes, sliding down her cheeks.

At that moment, the front door exploded open, banging against the wall behind it.

"Police! Get your hands up! Drop the weapon!"

Audrey used Jonathan's distraction to attempt to get away. But he grabbed her leg and hauled her back to him, throwing an arm around her shoulders, the knife again at her neck.

Three policemen stood in the doorway of the living room. Each one pointed a gun straight at Jonathan. "Let her go!" the officer in the middle shouted.

Jonathan's arm tightened against her neck. She felt the change in him, confidence melting to sudden uncertainty. "Jonathan, end this now," she said softly. "Please."

He pushed the knife blade against her throat. She sucked in a terrified breath.

"There's only one possible ending, Audrey," he said. "And you wrote it."

A click sounded from behind them, the safety of a gun being released. Audrey felt Jonathan stiffen in surprise.

"Let. Her. Go." The words deadly quiet.

Nicholas. Audrey blinked, an awful blend of hope and terror sweeping through her.

Jonathan laughed an unamused laugh. "I read your file, Wakefield. Webster did his homework. You think you're going to take me out and make up for that little sister you failed to protect? Isn't that what Audrey is to you? A chance to make up for what you broke?"

Audrey closed her eyes. "Jonathan, don't."

"You really are a son of a bitch, Colby," Nicholas said.

From the corner of her eye, Audrey saw Nicholas shove the gun against Jonathan's head. Jonathan jolted forward, then righted himself, keeping the knife at her neck.

"Don't!" Audrey screamed. "Don't do it, Nicholas. If you do, you'll be doing this his way. I never wanted that."

Heavy silence followed her words.

"Put the knife down, Mr. Colby," the police officer said again in a calm voice.

Audrey could feel the weight of Nicholas's struggle. "Please," she said. "Not like this."

An unbearable stretch of time passed before he pulled the gun away and said, "You're right. He's not worth it."

Jonathan relaxed. "I didn't think you had it in you, Wakefield."

In the next instant, Nicholas slammed the butt of the gun into Jonathan's head. He went limp and slumped to the floor.

CHAPTER SIXTEEN

AUDREY FELL to her knees, the dam inside her breaking, sobs shuddering through her. Nicholas dropped down beside her, pulled her into his arms and held her tightly, as if he could physically hold her together.

Two of the policemen handcuffed Jonathan, who had begun to come to.

Nicholas picked Audrey up, carried her outside where she sagged against the police car and pulled in ragged gasps of air.

The third police officer came out and clapped Nicholas on the shoulder, looked at Audrey and said, "Are you all right, ma'am?"

"Yes," she said, her voice a whisper.

"Are you sure?" Nicholas asked.

She nodded.

"He could have killed you," he said, anguish in his words.

"I never meant to drag you into this mess," she said, shaking her head.

"I think there's little question I willingly put myself here."

He wrapped his arms around her and held her against him. Audrey closed her eyes and welcomed the security. "He has to tell me where Sammy is," she said.

"Come on," Nicholas said, pulling her up beside him. "I have a feeling he may be ready to cooperate."

TWENTY MINUTES LATER, Nicholas banged on Ross's massive front door. Audrey stood just behind him. They'd said hardly anything on the drive here. Nicholas knew she needed to see her son, to know for herself that he was okay.

The door opened to an irritated Ross Webster. "Wakefield, what the hell—" His gaze swung to Audrey. He pressed his lips together. "I can't give him to you, Audrey."

Nicholas shoved Ross backward into the house. "The hell you can't. Where is Sammy?"

Ross's face blazed red with anger. "Get out of my house, Wakefield, or I'll call the police."

"They're a little tied up with Jonathan at the moment."

That stopped Ross cold.

Audrey ran to the bottom of the curving staircase in the foyer. "Sammy!" she called out. "Where are you?"

"Mama?"

Footsteps sounded in the hall above, and then Sammy was running down the stairs, catapulting into her arms.

"Oh, baby," Audrey sobbed, holding him to her.

Sammy pressed his face against her, clutching her neck. "Daddy said that you didn't want me to live with you anymore. That you were never coming back."

"Oh, Sammy, you're the most important thing in my life," she said, fighting back tears. "I will never leave you." She raised her head to look at Ross. "How could you do this?"

"He's Jonathan's son, too," Ross said, sounding less than convincing.

Audrey stared at him for a moment, then said, "I wonder if you'll feel the same when he does this to your daughter."

Ross went suddenly still, his face losing its color. "What are you talking about?"

"Maybe you should ask Laura," she said. And with that, she reached for Sammy's hand and walked out the door.

THEY STAYED at Nicholas's house that night. Exhausted, Sammy was asleep before Audrey left the room.

She found Nicholas in the kitchen, Lola at his feet, looking up at him with adoration. He'd gone to pick her up from his friend's house while Audrey showered and put Sammy to bed. He pulled the cork from a wine bottle now, then handed her a glass.

"Thank you," she said, taking a sip, and then adding, "for everything."

"You don't owe me any thanks."

"If you hadn't come when you did—"

"But I did," he said, his eyes intent on hers.

She dropped her gaze. "Yes. You did."

He set his glass on the counter, crossed the room and stopped in front of her, one hand cupping the back of her neck. "So where do we go from here?"

Audrey looked up at him, her heart full with emotion. She loved him and wanted him to know it. But timing was everything, or so the saying went. She could not offer him anything until she had her own life in order, figured out who she was without the specter of Jonathan's violence hanging over her. "I think we both have some loose ends that need tying up," she said.

He lifted her chin with a thumb. "If you decide there's a place for me in your life, then come and find me. That's all you have to do."

He leaned in and kissed her, and Audrey wondered if she were crazy to let him go. She kissed him back, and in her kiss let him know what she could not say.

EPILOGUE

The following spring

AUDREY DROVE with the windows down, the wind lifting her hair from the back of her neck. It was a beautiful Sunday afternoon in April. The trees were in full bloom, color was everywhere.

She'd dropped Sammy off at her parents' house that morning. He loved staying with them, loved going fishing with his grandpa, loved sitting at the kitchen table waiting for his grandma to pull a batch of cookies from the oven. The past year had given them time to get to know one another, and Audrey was unbelievably thankful for it.

For most of the three-hour drive, she stayed on secondary Georgia roads. It had always been her theory that you missed the good stuff on the Interstate.

She picked up a piece of paper from the passenger seat and checked her directions. The turn-off was just ahead on the right. Her stomach flipped. She should have called first.

It had been a year after all.

A year was a long time. A lot had happened.

For the most part, she felt as though she had a handle on her life. She would never be completely free of Jonathan. She hadn't once let herself think that she would. She'd handed the information Nicholas had given her over to the D.A., Kyle Travers, and that alone had earned Jonathan eighteen months in prison. Ross was serving a year and had been disbarred.

Six months ago, just after the divorce became final, Audrey had received a distraught phone call from Sylvia Webster, asking her to speak to Laura about Jonathan. They were getting married as soon as he was released. But Audrey knew that Laura saw in him what she wanted to see, and it wouldn't matter what she said to the younger woman. She would have to figure it out for herself.

Audrey hit her blinker now, turned onto the hard-top driveway and followed the tree-lined road a quarter mile or so until the trees gave way to fenced pasture. At the end of the road sat a stone farmhouse with twin magnolia trees in the front yard.

She stopped the Explorer and sat with her hands clenched on the steering wheel. A black-and-white dog bounced down the porch steps, barking. Audrey got out of the car, crouched down, and held out a hand. "Hey, Lola."

Lola's tail became a wagging blur.

A door opened. Audrey looked up. Nicholas stood on the top step of the porch, clearly surprised.

"Hey," she said, standing.

"Hey." He walked down the steps, his hands shoved in his pockets.

"I spoke to your parents," she said, feeling less certain of her decision to come now that she was here facing him. Maybe it was too late. "They told me where I could find you."

He stared at her for several long moments, not saying anything.

"How are you?" he asked finally, his eyes steady on hers.

"I'm good," she said. "Really good. And you?"

He nodded. "Yeah. Me, too."

Silence weighed heavy between them, and Audrey wondered again whether she should have come. "Could we talk?"

"Sure," he said. "Come in."

"How about out here? It's such a nice day."

He waved a hand at the porch. They crossed the yard and sat down on the steps.

"So how did you get all the way out here?" she asked, elbows propped on her knees.

"I decided the city wasn't for me. This farm belonged to my grandparents. No one's lived here for several years. My parents held onto it, hoping I would one day want it."

"They seem like very nice people."

"They are."

"Do you see them—"

"Yes," he said. "You were right. I had some loose ends of my own to take care of."

"I'm glad," she said.

"Me, too." He looked at her then, something between hope and uncertainty waging a struggle in his eyes. "I have to say I was beginning to think I would never see you again."

"This past year—it's had its rough spots. For a long time, I worried that I might lose Sammy because I took him out of the country. Jonathan's lawyers were of the pit-bull variety."

"It's all right?"

"Yes," she said. "And he's happy. Really happy. Playing soccer. And he's doing really well in school."

"That's great."

She nodded. "It is."

They fell into silence. Lola spotted a crow and darted after it, barking. The bird perched on a bottom limb of an apple tree, looked down and flapped its wings. Lola dropped onto the grass beneath the tree, panting.

"I can see she's busy these days," Audrey said.

"Oh, yeah. She has to keep the local wildlife in line."

Audrey smiled.

"So how about you?" he asked, his voice soft. "What have you done for you this past year?"

She looked down at her nails and rubbed her thumb across the back of her hand. "The first thing I did was to let myself admit I wasn't responsible for the direction my marriage took. For a long time, I blamed myself for not guessing how things would turn out, for not having the courage to find a way out sooner than I did. I started seeing this therapist, a woman who had been through something similar. She helped me a lot. I finally decided the blame and regret have no place in my life now. If anything, they're just an anchor to the past, and all I want is to sail on."

He reached out, covered her hand with his, squeezed once. Her heart sped up, and she felt the color rush to her cheeks.

On the fence at the edge of the yard, a pair of doves sat side by side. Audrey thought how right they looked there, how peaceful. It was the one thing she had yearned for—peace—and she had finally found it. But, undeniably, it hadn't been enough.

"I've missed you," she said.

"I missed you, too." They let the words sink in. And then he leaned over, his lips barely brushing her cheek. He pulled back and stared at her for a moment, as if reassuring himself of her presence. Something inside her collapsed with longing, and she kissed him back with all the feelings she'd kept locked away this past year.

She put her hands against his chest. He deepened the kiss, wrapping his arms around her. They kissed for a long time, reacquainting themselves, picking up where they'd left off. As if it were only yesterday. As if they had all the time in the world.

"I'm so glad you're here," he said, his voice uneven. He pushed her hair back from her face, his hand resting on her shoulder.

"I had to see who I was without all of the baggage from Jonathan. Find out whether I could be someone on my own."

"I know," he said. "And what did you decide?"

"That I can be. That I want more than just being on my own."

He looked at her, something warm and pleased in his eyes. "Does that mean there might be room for this? For us?"

A few seconds passed, and then she replied, "Yes. I think it does."

His grin was teasing. "Life with a small-town

lawyer with ambitions of running for district attorney. Word has it the guy lives on a farm and
doesn't know the first thing about farming."

She smiled. "So what kind of farming is he interested in?"

"Tomatoes. Green beans. Or so I hear."

"I've always wanted to grow watermelons,"
she said.

"Watermelons are good."

They were silent for a moment, eyes locked on
one another.

"Do you happen to have an extra shed anywhere around here?" she asked. "I kind of have a
little business going."

"As a matter of fact, I do."

"So," she said. "Maybe this could work."

"There's just one more thing I think we need
to be sure about first."

"Oh?" she asked. "What's that?"

"This kissing thing. That's pretty much got to
be right, or none of the rest will work."

"You have that on good authority?"

"Pretty good," he said.

"So maybe we'd better practice?"

"Highly advisable."

"Well," she said, lifting her shoulders, "I'm
available if you are."

He smiled and stood, holding out a hand. She

took it. He dropped an arm behind her knees, lifted her up and carried her inside the house, the screen door slapping closed behind them.

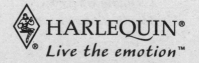

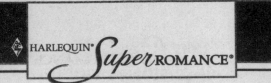

An Unlikely Match
by Cynthia Thomason

Harlequin Superromance #1312
On sale June 2005

She's the mayor of Heron Point. He's an
uptight security expert. When Jack Hogan
tells Claire Betancourt that her little town
of artisans and free spirits has a security
problem, sparks fly! Then her daughter goes
missing, and Claire knows that Jack is the
man to bring her safely home.

*Available wherever
Harlequin books are sold.*

If you enjoyed what you just read,
then we've got an offer you can't resist!

Take 2 bestselling love stories FREE!

Plus get a FREE surprise gift!

Clip this page and mail it to Harlequin Reader Service®

IN U.S.A.
3010 Walden Ave.
P.O. Box 1867
Buffalo, N.Y. 14240-1867

IN CANADA
P.O. Box 609
Fort Erie, Ontario
L2A 5X3

YES! Please send me 2 free Harlequin Superromance® novels and my free surprise gift. After receiving them, if I don't wish to receive anymore, I can return the shipping statement marked cancel. If I don't cancel, I will receive 6 brand-new novels every month, before they're available in stores. In the U.S.A., bill me at the bargain price of $4.69 plus 25¢ shipping and handling per book and applicable sales tax, if any*. In Canada, bill me at the bargain price of $5.24 plus 25¢ shipping and handling per book and applicable taxes**. That's the complete price, and a savings of at least 10% off the cover prices—what a great deal! I understand that accepting the 2 free books and gift places me under no obligation ever to buy any books. I can always return a shipment and cancel at any time. Even if I never buy another book from Harlequin, the 2 free books and gift are mine to keep forever.

135 HDN DZ7W
336 HDN DZ7X

Name	(PLEASE PRINT)	
Address	Apt.#	
City	State/Prov.	Zip/Postal Code

Not valid to current Harlequin Superromance® subscribers.

Want to try two free books from another series?
Call 1-800-873-8635 or visit www.morefreebooks.com.

* Terms and prices subject to change without notice. Sales tax applicable in N.Y.
** Canadian residents will be charged applicable provincial taxes and GST.
All orders subject to approval. Offer limited to one per household.
® are registered trademarks owned and used by the trademark owner and or its licensee.

SUPO4R   ©2004 Harlequin Enterprises Limited

Holiday to-do list:

- wrap gifts
- catch a thief
- solve a murder
- deal with Mom

Well-respected Florida detective Maggie Skerritt
is finally getting her life on track when a
suspicious crime shakes up her holiday plans.

Holidays Are Murder
Charlotte Douglas